LOVE IS

SUPERNATURAL

A Novel by

Janie De Coster

To submit a manuscript for our review,

email us at

submissions@majorkeypublishing.com

THE HUNT

The trio ran through the thick forest as fast as lighting, howling. It was mid-night; a full moon guided their path as they headed up the hill toward the castle, a night of terror laid upon the human race. Their blood-lust was legendary. The trio had fetched a total of sixty hearts and forty livers between them, which wasn't bad for a single night. They took from the young as well as the old, catching them unguarded. Their victims were traveling to and fro while others slept peacefully in their beds. Now, the deed was done as they made their way back to the dark river. At the edge, they threw the contents down and went into transition. Fur became skin, paws became hands as they returned to human form, shifting to an upright position. They then retrieved their clothing, which was hidden behind a tree a few feet away, along with an ice chest. They quickly dressed. The leader of the trio walked back to the contents and gathered them all. The second one opened the chest as the leader filled it. The third packed it all in. With the ice chest closed, they left the forest as men and woman.

SIX MONTHS LATER

Jerrico gazed out toward the magnificent courtyard as she stood on the balcony of the colossal castle she now called home. Acres of land led up to the castle, which sat boldly atop a hill. A long, cobblestone driveway lined with willow trees greeted every guest. The castle itself was taken right out of medieval times, with a drawbridge made of ancient wood. When Jerrico first laid eyes on the castle, she found it intriguing with its uniform grey stones of various shapes. She quickly realized her life would never be the same.

Jerrico was now the wife of Ashley Covington, a man of great wealth and prominence. She had to pinch herself every now and again to ensure she wasn't dreaming. He was a wonderful man, her real-life knight in shining armor. A little girl's princess dreams transformed into reality. But somewhere in the dark chambers of her heart, there was a fear brewing and she did not know why. Maybe it was just being in the castle itself that held a negative presence; yet Jerrico was fascinated by it. She had familiarized herself with nearly every cloistered room, of which there were many. Each one had a haunting feel. Even the walls themselves seemed to harbor ancient secrets of the past, and it was proven to her in a not so subtle way. Jerrico was told, in no uncertain terms by her new husband as well as the castle staff, of the rooms she was prohibited from entering. Jerrico recalled one particular day in the grand library, filled with hundreds and hundreds of centuries-old books. She had an unsettling experience with one of the castle's staff. Although she had been warned early on not to remove even a single book from its shelf, temptation got the best of her. Jerrico took in the rich covers of the various books as her eyes scanned the shelves, but there was one in particular that caught her eye, a crimson-colored book. Unfortunately, the book was too high on the shelf for her to reach. A step stool would be needed in order to achieve her task. Jerrico's eyes traveled around the room and landed upon one in the far corner of the room. She quickly sashayed across the room, grabbed the stool, and positioned it at the shelf where the book was stored. As she placed her right foot on the stool, the dead voice of Mr. John, the butler, filled the room.

"Mrs. Covington, I wouldn't do that if I was you."

Jerrico nearly jumped out of her skin as she took her feet off the stool and turned around to face him. Letting out a quickened breath, Jerrico said, "I just don't get it, Mr. John. What good is it to have such an array of lovely books if they can't be read by anyone?"

"Trust me, madame, it's all for the best," Mr. John said stiffly. He watched her closely with his dark, beady eyes. It was evident he wasn't going to leave the room until she did.

Jerrico quickly came to the conclusion that the Covington Manor was filled with dark secrets and mystery; certainly, that included the other people who occupied its dwelling as well. Even though her new husband treated her like a true princess and was very attentive to her needs, it did nothing to ease her fears.

Jerrico's mind revisited their whirlwind wedding. Ashley wanted them married right away. It seemed as if there was no talking him out of it. She barely had time to fly her mom and dad out to Miami from New York. Her cousin, Vivian, served as maid of honor as well as her wedding planner. In just one week, she and Ashley were husband and wife.

Although the wedding was thrown together so quickly, Vivian had done an exceptional job. Their wedding was deemed the wedding of the century. Over three hundred guests had attended. Everyone was elegantly dressed in dark designer suits and light-colored gowns. But there was something mystical and dark about all of them, even though their smiles appeared to be warm and normal. Maybe it was all in Jerrico's head, she rationalized. But it wasn't long before something else manifested itself, which validated her growing fears.

Just three weeks after her wedding, Jerrico began to notice some questionable things. The number three had been engraved in silver upon several of the doors throughout the castle. The castle's staff consisted of three maids, three butlers, and three cooks. There were three gardeners and three pool attendants as well. Still, according to Ashley, the number three meant absolutely nothing. It was all just a mere coincidence, from where her husband stood. But when, out of the blue, Ashley's mother, Cecelia–who, by the way, reminded her of Morticia from *The Addams Family*–informed her that she was expected to produce three babies within three years, she knew something unnatural was going on.

Jerrico didn't concern herself much with Cecelia's foolish wishes because she and Ashley had already discussed this very important subject on their wedding night. They weren't going to start planning for a family for at least four years. Ashley wasn't happy about waiting that long, but he went along with her request because he knew how important her career was to her. Jerrico's journey of becoming a lawyer was challenging. She worked her behind off to pass the bar, and now she was supposed to throw it all away, just so she could appease Ashley's mother? Absolutely not. It would be so silly of her and as far as Jerrico was concerned, her husband understood her position, and her mother-in-law would have to accept it as well.

Jerrico felt as if her head was still spinning like a merry-go-round from falling in love and marrying so quickly. Of course, she was as happy as any bride could be. But her gut was telling her that the ride she was on, as fantastic as it was, could get more completed than she ever imagined.

Jerrico felt the cool touch of Ashley's hand upon her shoulder, drawing her out of her thoughts as she stood on the balcony. It was her favorite place, overlooking the green landscape as the soft wind ruffled through her hair with its light breeze. As odd as it was, she'd never heard Ashley's footfalls as he entered or left a room, which was another thing about him that was quite disturbing. He made the cliché *light on his feet* true to a T.

"Honey, dinner is almost ready. You should come inside," he said with a gentle squeeze.

Jerrico turned and peered up into his emerald -green eyes. As much as she loved the color of them, she found them strange for a man of African descent; not to mention how intimidating they could be at times. Ashley was a good-looking man with bronze-colored skin and a strong, muscular physique that showed through the silk designer white shirt he wore. Jerrico had caught herself a prize, and she was so in love with him. Ashley had a mysterious aura that intrigued her and, at the same time, sent a shiver of fear through her veins. But she was known to have a predilection for *bad boys*; such was the case with her previous boyfriend, Sergen, who was quite a riot.

Jerrico turned around, pulling him into her. They kissed long and passionately. Catching their breath, Ashley whispered, "Wow, I'm famished in more ways than one." Jerrico knew exactly what he meant.

"And so am I. But first, let's take care of our hunger in the dining room." She chuckled lightly, leading the way.

The couple made their way down the long corridor, which led to the exquisite dining room. Ashley's parents, Zackery and Cecelia, were already seated at the long cherrywood dining table with a white Victorian style runner in the middle. Three sterling silver candelabras were lit, giving the atmosphere a formal glow. Zackery, the patriarch, was seated at the head of the table and his wife, Cecelia, sat to his right. Ashley, being the oldest of their children, sat at the opposite end of the table with Jerrico next to him. Winniford, Ashley's younger brother, was free to sit in whichever of the remaining eight chairs he preferred. This was the etiquette of the Covington's home. While Cecelia favored Morticia, her husband, Zackery, resembled the late actor Vincent Price, except for those emerald-green eyes. His voice was similar as well. It was deep and laced with mystery.

Jerrico didn't like the way her father-in-law looked at her. His eyes seemed to devour her. She felt that if she was a steak on his dinner plate, she would have been gone in minutes. It wasn't long before Mr. Hines the butler, a manas thin as a tooth pick walked into the room carrying trays of delicious food and drinks. As Jerrico received her food, she glanced over at Winniford, who was seated two chairs down from her. She had not noticed his arrival. It was an unsettling experience to have the seat completely empty one second and filled with a body the next. Her brother–in-law had his own issues that concerned her. She didn't like his sidelong glances. They weren't as intimidating as her father-in-law's, but just as annoying.

Fed up with the look he was giving her, Jerrico said, "Winniford, is there something you need to ask me?"

Winniford smiled slowly, giving her a firm and intense stare. "Not at all, my dear sister-in-law. I was just admiring how lovely you look tonight. My brother is a blessed man."

Winniford grinned. His comment threw her. How could she come back from such a complimentary gesture?

So she smiled politely and said, "Thank you, Winniford."

Obviously, Winniford wasn't as bashful as her husband had said.

Ashley had told Jerrico that Winniford was shy at heart, and something of an introvert. He only had a handful of dates under his belt, but he was definitely interested in finding the right woman to become his wife. Given his good looks, he should have no trouble attracting women, Jerrico thought. Winniford was just as handsome as his older brother; a carbon copy, in fact. The only difference existed in height and color. Winniford stood a few inches shorter and was a shade lighter, but they shared the same emerald-colored eyes. Any woman in her right mind would have been delighted to be in his presence, Jerrico thought. Just like her husband, Winniford had a mysterious aura about him. It was an aura that said *approach with extreme caution.* Maybe that warning sign was the culprit to keeping that special woman away. Maybe she too should have paid closer attention to that flashing sign. But it was too late now.

Jerrico was very cautious of her mother-in-law, Cecelia. Jerrico's eyes traveled across the table, landing on her mother-in-law's face. Cecelia's skin was extremely smooth for a woman of her particular age; her long black hair hung loosely over her shoulders and down the designer black dress she wore. Jerrico thought her whole wardrobe consisted of the color black. She never saw the woman in anything else, even at her and Ashley's wedding. She wore a fabulous designer gown which was almost a carbon copy of what Angelina Jolie wore in the movie *Maleficent*. Cecelia also had a perfect set of white teeth. Jerrico wondered whether they were her own or an expensive set of veneers because they were so bright, you had to almost squint when you looked at her. Cecelia smiled brightly and often, but the sunshine smile never seemed to reach her eyes. Cecelia took a sip of her red wine and returned the silver flute to the leaf-shaped coaster. Cecelia interrupted her thoughts.

"Jerrico, why do you always look as if you've seen a ghost whenever Winniford comes to the table?" Cecelia asked, flashing that sunshine smile.

If your son moved around like a regular person, I wouldn't look scared out of my wits, Jerrico thought.

Jerrico lowered her eyes from Cecelia's blinding stare and said, "He moves like a fox. One moment, you don't see him and the next, he's here."

Winniford gave Jerrico another sidelong glance she found annoying and said, "Correction, Jerrico, I assure you I am much quicker than a fox." He chuckled.

Winniford's eyes gleamed as he stared at her yet again. Jerrico turned her head, shunning his shifty eyes. She fixed her eyes onto her plate. She never looked over at him again. His very appearance made her uncomfortable. The same could be said of the other Covingtons as well, including her husband, Ashley.

The food tasted delicious, as always. They dined on baked chicken, rice pilaf, and fresh garden greens with a side salad that could be considered a normal meal on any given night of the week in America. What disturbed Jerrico was the fact that the family ate tons of raw meat. There was always rare steak or raw liver on the menu, no matter what else was being served. Jerrico thought of herself as a well-rounded woman, but never had she seen a custom such as this. Jerrico watched in awe as Winniford reached over with the fork he held, stuck it into the bloody piece of meat that was on a platter, and placed it on his plate. With the knife, he sliced off a piece and put it in his mouth. His eyes seemed to light up as he chewed. Ashley and his family conversed like your average family, sharing their typical day's events, but Jerrico knew there was nothing average about them.

"Jerrico dear, it nearly slipped my mind but you had a phone call earlier today, when you were out."

"Oh?" Jerrico responded with a raised brow. She placed her fork onto her plate and waited for her mother-in-law to continue.

"It was from Mr. Frost, from Taylor & Frost Law Firm," Cecelia said, displaying just a hint of her blinding smile. "I believe you have an interview scheduled with them tomorrow."

She reached her long, red manicured nails into the china bowl and selected a piece of raw liver. Bringing it back to her dish, she sliced into it with the butter knife. She lifted the meat to her mouth, but paused to speak again.

"I told them I wasn't so sure if you were still interested."

Jerrico watched with eyes stretched as Cecelia popped the liver into her mouth and chewed ever so slowly. Jerrico gulped. A wave of nausea washed over her, but she quickly recovered. Jerrico slowly began to steam after hearing the words that came out of Cecelia's mouth. In her head, she pondered the best way to handle this: like the lady her mother raised her to be? Or should she go with her more aggressive side and beat her down like a bully in the street? She decided to make her mother proud. Taking in a breath, she spoke in the most level tone she could muster.

"Cecelia, why in heaven's name would you tell them that? I am very much interested in the position. You do know how hard I worked to get this interview?" She struggled to keep the anger out of her voice.

Cecelia kept her cool. She placed the remaining piece of the slippery meat into her mouth, chewing slowly as if she wasn't under attack.

"I am sorry, my dear, but have you considered the responsibilities you now have as a new bride, along with being a Covington? There will be charity events you are expected to attend, not to mention The Women Auxiliary Club, along with others. My dear, I believe your plate to be full," she said without an ounce of remorse.

Jerrico dismissed Cecelia's explanation. "I will call them back first thing in the morning and assure them I will keep the interview," Jerrico said, letting out a frustrated sigh as she pushed her dish aside.

Cecelia's comment and complete lack of concern caused her appetite to dissipate. But this wasn't their first discrepancy.

Jerrico and Cecelia had butted heads right from the start. Cecelia had chastised Jerrico for everything, from the way she dressed to the way she spoke to her son. She was the perfect example of the mother-in-law from hell. And her husband had never even tried to defend her not once. *This is too much*, Jerrico thought as she peered over at Ashley. And sure enough, he continued to eat as if nothing had transpired between the two.

"I've had enough. I'm going to bed," she muttered, getting up from the table with a jolt, which brought Ashley out of his trance.

"Jerrico, honey, come back," Ashley said as he reached out and gently grabbed her by the arm.

"No, Ashley," she said, wiggling her arm free from his grasp. "I'll see you upstairs."

Jerrico prepared for bed as Ashley showered alone. Rarely did they take showers together, even though they were still newlyweds. It was a pet peeve of Ashley's which, of course, she did not understand. What natural born, red-blooded man would not want a naked woman in his shower? But her husband was a different man and she accepted his unfamiliar ways. All in all, they loved each other and that was all that mattered. Jerrico still had to pinch herself as she looked around the luxurious bedroom. Thick red and gold carpeting covered the floor. The king-sized bed with Victorian-style post in the middle of the room with rich, thick gold bedding upon it. Turning back the plush comforter Jerrico lay upon the golden cotton sheets. Letting out a tired yawn, she closed her eyes as her mind revisited the dialog during dinner. In spite of the appearance of enjoying each other's company, she couldn't help but notice a chill in the room that even the warm flicker of the candles couldn't remove. But what Cecelia had said to her earlier warmed her up quite well.

The tiff with her mother-in-law lingered in Jerrico's mind as she lay in bed. Cecelia knew she was trying to land a secure position here in Miami since she left her job back in New York. Was she deliberately trying to sabotage her efforts? Jerrico was doing her best to get along with her in-laws, but this was just another event that made it almost impossible.

Ashley stepped out of the shower wrapped in his signature white robe. She barely saw him completely naked in the light. Ashley preferred darkness when they made love. Even though she was still pissed, looking at her handsome husband dispelled the anger within her. Sexual hunger took over as she lifted her head from the pillow and met his eyes.

Ashley removed his robe and slid underneath the covers. He placed a lingering kiss on her lips as his hand ran across the firmness of her breast, sending an electric spark through her body.

"Honey, I want to apologize for Mother's thoughtlessness. She meant no harm," he whispered as his tongue teased the tip of her ear and traveled down to the crevice of her neck. "I spoke with her and she apologized. She assured me she would never do that again."

Jerrico knew Cecelia's apology wasn't sincere. But it made her happy to know that, for once, her husband had come to her defense.

"Apology accepted, Ashley," she said breathlessly as she succumbed to the desires taking over her body.

The Model Cousin

Vivian answered her cell on the third ring. She was at her studio watching three lean models prance before her on the catwalk, showcasing her colorful designs. Vivian had a fashion show in a few weeks and wanted nothing but the best for the buyers from California and New York. Waving her hand for the ladies to take a break, Vivian swung her long brunette weave over her shoulder and answered the call.

"Hello, Luv," she greeted Jerrico.

"Hello, Viv. You won't believe what that hideous mother-in-law of mine did last night," Jerrico began.

From the tone of her cousin's voice, Vivian knew something had gone terribly wrong yet again at the Covington's.

"What is it, Jerri?" Vivian asked, taking a seat in one of the folding steel chairs lined against the studio wall.

Jerrico let out a whiff of air, even though her anger toward Cecelia had subsided a bit, thanks to the fact that she was able to salvage the interview. She had called Mr. Frost early this morning and assured him she wanted that interview as much as she needed her next breath. Everything was set. She would be meeting with him at ten-thirty. Jerrico went on to explain the manipulation of Cecelia Covington.

"Come on Jerri, I'm sure the old woman wasn't trying to undermine you. The poor dear is probably lonely in that big old dusty castle of hers and wants to keep you under feet for a while. Cut her some slack, Jerri." Vivian chuckled.

Viv was always the diplomatic one and an expert at sizing things up; once again, Jerrico felt better about the situation. Vivian might be on point. Maybe she was overreacting, considering all the new changes she had been going through lately.

"Well, I'll let her off the hook this time but she needs to stop pushing my buttons." Jerrico huffed.

"Jerrico the New Yorker with a short fuse," Vivian teased.

"Viv, after my interview, do you think we can meet for lunch?"

"Why certainly, Jerri, but I will have to get right back to work. I got a show coming up this weekend, and I'm tearing my weave to pieces to make it wonderful."

"That's fine, Viv and I know it will be as smashing as always. I'll ring you when I'm done." Jerrico paused. "Viv."

"Yes, Jerri."

"Never mind," Jerrico said, ending their call.

There was something else she wanted to talk to her cousin about, but Jerrico wasn't even sure if Vivian had a solution for her. In the meantime, her focus had to be on landing the position at Taylor & Frost.

The Interview

Jerrico dressed in a tailor made, navy blue, two-piece pant suit with a navy Christian Dior bag on her shoulder, along with matching red-bottom heels. She strolled into the three-story office building of Taylor & Frost. Jerrico noticed the décor of the office, with its white walls and modern grey and black furniture. An array of exotic plants were scattered about, giving the room a welcoming feel. On the foyer wall hung two large oil paintings, one of Mr. Taylor and the other of Mr. Frost. Jerrico continued down the short hall to approach the receptionist desk.

A young, light-skinned woman with full, coffee-colored eyes greeted her with a smile.

"You must be Mrs. Jerrico Covington." She perked.

Jerrico felt a little awkward. The lady didn't give her a chance to introduce herself. But that wasn't out of the ordinary. She could have been the only one scheduled today for an interview. So why was this uneasiness forming in the pit of her stomach?

"Yes I am, and I'm here for an interview with…"

"Yes, with Mr. Frost. He will be with you shortly," the receptionist interjected as she pointed to a seat near the window.

"Thank you," Jerrico said as she walked over to the appointed chair.

"By the way, my name is Dana," the receptionist announced, getting up from the desk and walking down the long hallway toward three office doors. She entered the third one.

Jerrico scanned the lobby. Those oil paintings seemed to be drawing her attention like a magnet. She stood and walked over to them. She studied the distinguished faces in the paintings. Both gentlemen wore black suits, white shirts, and grey ties which complemented the black and white look of the office. What captured Jerrico's attention more pointedly was their eyes. They were emerald- green, the same color that her husband and in-laws shared. A chill ran down her spine like ice water.

"Mrs. Covington?" a deep, rich voice said behind her.

Jerrico jumped at the sound.

"I'm sorry, did I scare you?" Mr. Frost said in a gentle tone.

"Um...no," Jerrico stuttered as she turned.

"I'm Mr. Frost," he said, extending his hand.

Jerrico took it and looked into his eyes. She felt the temperature in her body rise while the temperature of his hand was quite cool. The same emerald-green eyes from the paintings stared back at her.

"Follow me," he said as he let go of her hand.

They walked into the third office. Jerrico took in the layout. There were two floor-to-ceiling windows showing the spectacular view of the city. There were three beautiful oil–stained paintings hung evenly on the wall. Jerrico lowered her eyes. Mr. Frost took a seat behind his black, square glass table with three stacks of paperwork neatly stacked upon it. And yes, three single chairs aligned neatly in front of the desk in which Jerrico was invited to take a seat. She couldn't help but notice this phenomenon of threes. And oddly enough, thirteen minutes later. she was welcomed aboard with Taylor & Frost.

Jerrico was floating on cloud nine as she and Mr. Frost shook hands once more before she left the office. As she strolled past the receptionist, she gave her a quick wave goodbye.

But before Jerrico made it out of the lobby, the smiling receptionist said, "Looking forward to seeing you on Monday. Nine O'clock sharp, Mrs. Covington!"

Jerrico was taken aback. How did she instinctively know her starting date and time?

Jerrico stopped mid-step, turned her head, and stood completely still. Clutching the chain of her navy bag, she found herself staring at the woman. She could have sworn her eyes were brown when she first laid eyes on her, but now they were emerald-green. Like her husband, his family, Mr. Frost, and Mr. Taylor.

"Are you okay, Mrs. Covington?"

Jerrico swallowed hard as her heart began to pound. She needed fresh air. "Yes, I'm fine. See you on Monday at nine," she uttered, hurrying out the door.

Jerrico took in a deep breath before she galloped across the parking lot. She looked over her shoulder a couple times as she went. Not only was she reeling from what she just experienced; now, she had this eerie feeling that she was being watched. Her cell rang as she reached her black Infinity. Hitting the button, she unlocked the door and slid inside. She fished into the Chanel bag and pulled out her phone. It was her husband.

"Hi, Ashley, I didn't expect to hear from you so soon."

"Well, honey, I just wanted to see how the interview had gone," he said in a warm, but guarded voice.

"Honey, I got the job!" she squealed. "Somebody upstairs must have put in a really good word for me because it felt like a walk in the park. I will start on Monday. How great is that?" she chimed. Jerrico kept her voice light, in spite of her frazzle nerves. She decided to keep the unusual incident between her and Dana, the receptionist, to herself for now.

"Well, in honor of that news, I would love to take my wife out to dinner. Can you meet me at *660 at The Anglers,* say around six? You do know how to get there?"

"Mmm, I think so but I'll set the GPS anyway," Jerrico responded.

"Good, I'll see you then," Ashley said.

"Honey, wait," Jerrico said just before he hung up. "Just so you know, I'm having lunch with Vivian. You know it's been a while since we spent some time together."

"That's fine, just stay in town. It doesn't make sense for you to drive all the way back to the country when you are already in the city."

"But then you will have to come here to the city, and we will have two cars to drive back instead of just one."

Ashley had worked from home today, so he was at the castle.

"Don't you worry about that, honey. You just go on and meet with Vivian and I'll see you soon. Love you."

"Love you, too." Jerrico smiled.

Well, at least Ashley sounded happy that I got the job, she thought. Her fear had been that his mother may have gotten in his head. Jerrico knew Cecelia was used to getting her way, but not this time. Now, she would have something else to focus on instead of her in-laws and their ominous ways. She started the car, programmed her GPS, and pulled out of the parking lot and into traffic.

Keeping Secrets

Vivian poured over the fashion designs in her portfolio after getting off the phone with her cousin, Jerrico. She hoped whatever else her cousin had in mind would have nothing to do with the Covingtons. They were a dangerous topic. Vivian had dodged one bullet already with Cecelia's careless mishandling of that call to Mr. Frost. Hopefully, there wasn't another issue lurking around the corner that she would have to deal with. As Vivian flipped through the designs, her mind took a step back in time. She remembered her life back in New York City. Growing up, she was a happy kid. She had great parents, lots of friends, and a cousin whom she adored like a sister. She and Jerrico were very ambitious. They wanted to take the world by its tail. So they made a pact when they were young that they would go after their dreams, no matter what obstacle came their way and after all these years, they had done just that.

Vivian's modeling dream had come true in spades. She was a model in high demand. Her good looks and slender body landed her on the covers of several major magazines throughout the country. She traveled extensively around the world and worked with the most rich and famous people. Jerrico was also a beautiful young woman, with light caramel-colored skin, hazel doe-like eyes and an oval face. She could have been a model also, but Jerrico had chosen the field of law. But when it came to love, they each had their share of rollercoaster rides. Vivian had ditched her previous beau, Charlie Dole, who was a narrow-minded control freak.

Jerrico finally saw the light when it came to that cheating scoundrel she had dated, Sergen Reynolds. Actually, Vivian had a secret she was keeping. Sergen never cheated on Jerrico, but she had to make it look that way. She knew what was best for her cousin, and it wasn't him. She wanted–no, needed Jerrico in her circle. And Vivian was happy she did it. Jerrico had married a wonderful man. *Ashley Covington is perfect for her*, Vivian thought. Not only was Jerrico's love life thriving since she'd met Ashley Covington, Vivian's life has been out of this world as well since meeting the new man in her life, Max Parker. A lifetime of happiness was in store for her and Jerrico. She was certain of it.

Lunch With A View

Jerrico walked into Alfresco, located near the beach. It was a place where patrons could dine and take in the view of the ocean. When Jerrico walked through the semi-crowded eatery, she found her cousin's head bent over her drawings at a table near the end of the dock.

"Hi there," Jerrico said.

Vivian stood to greet her with a hug and air kisses, and then they took their seats.

"You are always working," Jerrico scolded, looking down at the portfolio.

"Great designs, cousin," she mused as her eyes fell on a lovely shell-colored pants suit on the canvas.. "You like?"

"Yes, it's beautiful!" Jerrico exclaimed.

"Maybe you'll find it under the tree at Christmas," Vivian teased.

Jerrico hung her designer bag with a long bronze chain over the corner of the metal chair and folded her hands on the table. Vivian was always gifting her with her exceptional designs on birthdays, Christmas, and sometimes just because.

"Vivian, you spoil me relentlessly."

Vivian closed the portfolio and said, "I love buying you things. You're my little sister and I want only the best for you, Jerri." Vivian reached out and cupped Jerrico's chin. "I love you."

"I know, Viv, and I love you for it," Jerrico replied with a smile. Vivian dropped her hand and leaned back in her seat. "I ordered an Italian Chop Salad with ranch dressing and a dirty martini for us. Is that okay?"

"You always know what I like," Jerrico said with a chuckle.

"Yes, Jerri, I know what interests you. We are like two peas in a pod. Or, should I say a yin and a yang?" Vivian laughed and Jerrico joined in.

"I will always look out for my girl, and I hope you will remember that no matter what happens in the future, it's coming from a good place," Vivian said with a serious expression on her face.

Jerrico didn't quite understand the statement coming from Vivian, and it made her a little uncomfortable.

"Vivian, you're being a little weird right now," Jerrico said with a tilt of her head.

A red-headed waiter who resembled a young Clay Aiken from American Idol brought their salads and drinks, then placed their dishes before them.

Vivian didn't respond to Jerrico's observation. She decided to get down to what was really on Jerrico's mind. "So, what do you need to talk to me about, Jerri?" Vivian asked.

Jerrico moved the lettuce around on her plate as she contemplated how to broach this daunting subject. She had no desire to come across as a mental case. But so many strange things were occurring and it was driving her bananas.

Vivian saw her hesitation and said, "Jerri, whatever it is just, say it."

Jerrico put her fork down, folded her hands on the table, and started, "Viv, I hope you don't think I've lost some of my marbles, but there is something strange going on at the Covington Castle."

Vivian picked up her drink and took a sip. Lowering the glass, she asked, "Can you be more specific?"

Before Vivian could say another word, Jerrico blurted it out. "Vivian, I believe the castle is haunted, and the people in it...well, I'm not sure what they are, but they are certainly not of this world."

Vivian paused and a whimsical look appeared on her face.

"To which I then would say...my golly, you may be right on both accounts, Jerri." Vivian's perfectly done eyebrows raised just a little as she stared at her cousin. "The Covingtons are eccentric people, and their decades old castle may very well have some strange occurrences floating around, wouldn't you think?"

Jerrico gave her a thousand-yard stare. Of course, she knew the Covingtons were on a different level than most people she had the opportunity to have met, and yes castles most likely were haunted, but this was something a little more sinister.

"I wish I *had* seen a ghost. That would have been so much easier to explain," she responded, letting out a deep breath. "But no, Viv. I got a feeling there is more to it than ghosts running around, and it scares me to my very soul."

Vivian saw that her cousin didn't respond to her lighthearted statement as she hoped she would. Jerrico was really alarmed, so she quickly decided another approach…appeasing her fears.

"I see that you are clearly moved by this. So tell me, in depth, what happened, Jerri," Vivian said, picking up a forkful of salad.

Just as she did, a waiter walked by carrying a plate with a rare steak for another patron. Vivian could almost see the blood oozing out of it with her keen eyesight. Her eyes followed the young man as he placed the diner plate upon the table across from where they sat. Vivian's mouth watered as she swallowed the salad in her mouth. Her pulse quickened as her tongue moved around in her mouth, craving the taste of the bloody liquid. The salad before her had now lost its appeal. She wanted the taste of blood so badly, she was tempted to go over there and just take it.

"Vivian? Vivian?" Jerrico said, breaking her out of her trance. Vivian turned her head quickly to face her. Her face clearly flushed. "Why were you staring at that waiter? Do you know him?" Jerrico asked, clueless as to what was really going on with her cousin.

"Um no," Vivian said with a shake of her head. She picked up her fork and pitched a wad of chop salad into her mouth, hoping to get rid of her desire for blood. Chewing quickly, she said, "I thought I may have seen him before, but it was a mistake."

Jerrico thought Vivian was acting strangely, seeing the expression on her face and the way her eyes kept darting over to the other patron's plate. However, she moved on with her story.

"Vivian, the way those Covingtons and the staff move around...I'm tellin' you, you never hear their footfall, ever, Viv. It's eerie. One moment, you're completely alone in a room and with a blink of an eye, they're standing right behind you. It's downright creepy, Viv." Jerrico chimed as she let out a breath.

Vivian nodded her head, but didn't say a word as Jerrico continued.

"I feel eyes following me around all the time, and that doesn't include shadows I see out of the corner of my eyes." Jerrico took a sip of her martini. Her nerves flared just talking about it.

"Have you brought this to your husband's attention?" Vivian asked, never looking up from her plate.

"Viv, Ashley is included in the things I've just told you. I can't even hear my own husband's footsteps when he walks into a room. It's like he's also walking on freakin' air."

Jerrico realized her voice had rose a decibel. She leaned forward in her seat and said in a lower tone, "Look, I know I'm sounding like some crazy woman, but I swear to you I'm telling you the truth."

Vivian took Jerrico's hand into hers and said, "Calm down, Jerri. I know this is upsetting to you, but I'm sure all of it has a reasonable explanation."

Jerrico quickly pulled her hand out of Vivian's and leaned back in her seat. She noticed how cool her cousin's fingers were. *Just like Mr. Frost's and Ashley,* she mused silently.

"You don't believe me, do you?"

"Jerri, that's not it at all. Now, you just think about it for a moment. You're an occupant in a century-old castle and, like I mentioned earlier, you are bound to feel or hear things that are questionable. It's all natural, Jerrico. Your nerves are just getting the best of you right now, my dear. Maybe you should see someone…a physician." Vivian's voice was warm as she continued, "I don't believe you are a crazy woman, maybe a scared one, but certainly not crazy. Please make an appointment and get a little something to help you sleep, that's all."

Jerrico took a long sip of her wine. Setting the glass down, she said. "Well, maybe you're right. A city girl in an old Victorian style castle is a setup for the supernatural."

"Now, that's a closing argument for a real case. You're not studying those law books for nothing." Vivian laughed.

"Vivian, I'm so glad you're my cousin. I'm also grateful that I accepted your invitation to come out here to Miami. That decision has changed my life. Overall, I'm happy, Viv. And I will see a doctor as you suggested." Jerrico smiled.

Vivian took her hand again. This time, they were warm, Jerrico noticed.

"Well, I'm happy to hear that. "And *I have every intention of keeping you that way,* Vivian thought as she looked into Jerrico's smiling face.

Surprise!

Jerrico entered the dimly lit restaurant and was guided to the table by the maître d'. A breath caught in her throat as she scanned the faces of the Covington family. It was not only her husband, Ashley, that greeted her, but Winniford and their parents were seated around the table as well.

"Surprise!" they all chimed. Cecelia's blinding smile didn't quite light up the room as it was usually known to do.

Ashley pulled out Jerrico's chair and she took her seat. She was almost speechless.

"Honey, you could have told me everyone was going to be here," Jerrico said, still trying to get over the Covingtons being present.

"Everyone is not here yet," Winniford said, giving her one of his familiar sidelong glances.

"Who else is coming?" Jerrico asked as Vivian suddenly appeared behind her back.

"Do you think I would miss out on celebrating your success, Jerri?" Vivian said, reaching out and giving her a warm hug.

Vivian then took her seat as the waiter brought over a tray of drinks.

Ashley lifted his glass and made a toast. "To my lovely wife, I wish you much success in your new career!"

"Here! Here!" they all said as their glasses touched.

Jerrico scanned the table. Their emerald-green eyes glimmered as they looked at Jerrico, even Vivian's, yet Jerrico knew that from birth, Vivian's eyes were black.

An Evening Walk

Later that evening, Jerrico decided to go for a leisurely walk on the grounds. The day's events weighed heavily on her mind. Maybe a long walk would do her some good. She needed some perspective and a good night's sleep. Lately, she found herself tossing and turning until the wee hours of the morning. It was a nice, warm evening as she followed the familiar path she and Ashley would walk together. The stars shined like little diamonds in the sky. She didn't mind walking alone because the Covingtons' guards were in charge of keeping the grounds safe and secured. Ashley remained in the study. He and his father were on a conference call with one of their associates in France. Secretly, Jerrico was relieved. She wanted to be alone for a while.

The events of the day played around in her head. *How did Ashley arrange for everyone to meet at the restaurant so quickly,* she mused. In Vivian's case, she said she had a photo shoot she needed to get back to right after they met for lunch, and it was supposed to last for hours. Of course, she could have been giving her a snow job to conceal what was really going on. And then there were the Covingtons. Were they really happy she had gotten hired, or was it just a ruse to keep her off guard? Every weird thing came floating back into her mind as she strolled. And what about the receptionist at Taylor & Frost? How did she know so quickly that she had the position? Did Mr. Frost call her desk and inform her in the minutes it took her to reach the lobby?

"There I go, over-analyzing everything again," she whispered to herself.

The path she took from the castle was well lit. She had followed the cobblestones all the way out to the grassy area of the ground as if she was Dorothy in the *Wizard of Oz*. Jerrico gazed at each willow tree as she walked. When she reached the seventh tree, Jerrico noticed something a little disturbing. The branch of the tree had taken a peculiar form. Jerrico stood before the willow and studied it. The branch was shaped like the number three. Jerrico blinked several times as she stared at it. She couldn't believe her very own eyes. She had seen many trees in her day, but never one with such a deformity. Stepping closer to the tree, she reached out and traced the branch with the tip of her finger. As she did, a gust of wind appeared out of nowhere, blowing the mid-length floral print skirt she wore up over her knees. Jerrico dropped her hands and placed them onto her skirt and held it down. She tried to take a step, but she couldn't move. Her feet seemed to be planted in the ground right where she stood. She continued to stare at the deformed branch as the wind grew stronger, to the point of making her sway from side to side. But she still wasn't able to move her feet.

Suddenly, she felt hands on the back of her neck. She let go of her flaring skirt and a harrowing scream ripped from the bottom of her throat. It was then that she regained the movement of her legs. She quickly turned around to see who was behind her. Seeing no one, Jerrico's eyes grew wider. She placed her hand frantically over her head. *What is happening to me*, she thought as the wind powerfully swirled around her. She didn't expect a storm tonight. In fact, she could have sworn the weather man had predicted a clear, starry night. Jerrico looked up. The sky had darkened and was absent of the beautiful stars that had guided her earlier. Now, the wind not only grew stronger, it began to get colder.

Jerrico took off running, but pebbles of sand were getting into her eyes, obstructing her vision and making it difficult for her to see. Jerrico's eyes squinted into slits as she forced them to focus. She ran and ran as fresh tears slid down her cheeks. She felt as if she was running up a steep hill as the wind pushed violently against her.

"Help!" she cried out as the wind now grew bone-chilling cold. Jerrico's cheeks began to sting as if they were pricked with little needles. For a brief moment, Jerrico wondered where the guards were, but it was a passing thought. Her whole focus now was to make it to safety as she wrestled with the ferocious wind.

Finally, she was able to make it to the drawbridge of the castle, and then to the steps leading to its entryway. Jerrico wrapped her arms around one of the columns as the wind continued to howl. Her hair wrapped around her face, like a scarf blocking her view as she cried relentlessly.

"Someone, please, help me please!" she screamed as loud as she could.

She let go of the column and began to inch her way over to the castle's door. The wind wasn't letting up. It fought against her with every determined step she made.

Then, as suddenly as the wind started, it came to a screeching halt. Jerrico stood on the porch, stunned as she pulled her disheveled hair out of her face. She turned toward the front door and let out a piercing scream as a tall, dark figure stood before her.

"Jerrico, it's me, Winniford. What is the matter with you?" he asked, looking at her as if she just lost her mind. "Look at you. Where have you been?"

Jerrico caught her breath and replied, "I was caught in a terrible storm. The wind was so strong, I could hardly make it back to the castle. I can't believe no one heard me screaming. Where are the guards, Winniford?"

Winniford didn't answer. He looked around and then glanced up at the sky.

"Jerrico, there isn't any storm."

Jerrico felt tears forming in her eyes as she followed his gaze.

"Winniford, there was a storm. Look at me!" Jerrico exclaimed with flared arms. She took a step forward. "The wind was strong and it kept pushing me backward, and then it became freezing, as if it was winter. I had to fight with everything in me to make it back to the castle."

Jerrico's eyes widened as the castle door opened and Ashley stepped out. Taking one look at his wife, he pulled her into his arms.

"Honey, where were you and are you alright?"

Jerrico began to weep as she fell into his arms and clung to him.

"I got caught up in a bitter storm, Ashley. The wind was so strong and cold," she sputtered as Ashley stroked her hair.

"Honey, what are you talking about? There's no storm."

Jerrico let go of him and looked around once more. The wind had ceased and the sky was scattered with twinkling stars. The moon shone brightly. In fact, the weather was just as it was when she began her walk. Jerrico thought the universe was mocking her. She had gone through a storm. It was real. *It just had to be, or else I'm really losing my mind,* she thought. Suddenly, her knees grew weak and she began to sway. Ashley quickly placed his arms around her.

"Come on, honey. Let me get you inside," Ashley said as he guided her into the castle.

Winniford took off into the night with a bountiful wind behind him, a wind that was accustomed to his kind.

I Can See Clearly Now

The following morning at the breakfast table, the Covingtons were seated in their respective seats. An impressive spread of bacon, eggs, buttermilk pancakes, and fresh brewed coffee adorned the table. Jerrico's stomach growled as she dove into her food. Her unsettling experience the previous night had brought on an intense appetite. She ate in silence as she listened to the banter of the family. Then, Winniford spoke up.

"Jerrico had an eventful evening. Do you care to tell the family about your experience?"

No, I don't care to tell the family. But I do care to throw this hot coffee in your face, she mused silently. Jerrico was certain that Winniford had something to do with what had happened to her, even though she knew he didn't have the power to control the weather. Jerrico lowered her head.

In a small voice she said, "No, I don't."

Zackery peered up from the morning paper and said, "I would like to know what happened. Does anyone other than Jerrico care to fill me in?"

Ashley cleared his throat and said, "It's nothing to worry about, Father. My wife just went out for a little walk at dusk. She believed she came upon a storm at some point, which frightened her.

"It was probably one of those strange storms that pops up now and again," Winniford cut in as he took a bite of his fruit.

"That's what I thought, too," Ashley agreed and turned to look over at his wife. "It scared the wits out of her, but she's okay now. Aren't you, dear?" He chimed as he rubbed the top of her hand.

It was supposed to be a comforting gesture; however, it did nothing to calm her. Jerrico lifted her head to see eight sets of emerald eyes staring at her.

"Yes, I'm just fine. No one needs to worry," she said tightly.

"Well, that's good to hear, my dear," Cecelia said, flashing a lackluster smile.

Jerrico could see that not one of them believed her. *Or, maybe they did. Maybe it was a mind game they were all playing to send her over the deep end*, Jerrico thought. The family returned to their activities at the table as Mr. John walked in carrying the cups of liver Zackery and Cecelia ate at breakfast, lunch, and dinner. Sometimes, Ashley would take a bite or two and so would Winniford. Jerrico had had enough of pretending everything was normal in the Covington household. She was through with talking herself out of every strange thing that she saw or felt.

Jerrico cleared her throat and said in a loud, agitated voice, "You know, I am not alright. It wasn't just a stupid little storm that upset me last night. It was a terrifying one. And it didn't come upon me until I touched that deformed branch of the seventh willow tree!" Jerrico screamed. The Covington clan gasped all at once.

They watched her outburst with completely blank faces as they waited for her next move. Jerrico raised her hand and pointed her finger at each one of them.

"You all know it's out there. It's not natural, and it needs to be removed right away," Jerrico said through tight lips. Cecelia was the first to respond to Jerrico's request. She threw back her head and let out a chuckle so deep, it sounded as if it was coming from the dungeon.

"Dear, there is no such tree on this property." She grinned

"There most certainly is, Cecelia." Jerrico rebuffed. "I touched it with this finger," Jerrico challenged, wiggling it. Cecelia peered over at her husband and then to her sons. With a profound expression on her face, she looked at her daughter-in-law. "I'm not afraid to say it, my dear, but I believe you're starting to lose touch." Cecelia smirked.

Jerrico's eyes narrowed, peering into the face of her twisted mother-in-law. Was she suggesting that she wasn't aware of truth or reality?

Ashley cleared his throat. He wasn't going to let his mother pre-diagnose his wife with a mental illness he knew wasn't vital.

"Mother, Jerrico is fine. She was out there in the dark and all alone. It's easy to see how she may have gotten confused, but she's home now safe and sound," Ashley consoled as he gave his mother a *let it go* stare.

Jerrico shook her head in protest. "Yes, I am here now, but know what I saw, Ashley. I'm not imagining things," Jerrico replied.

"Nobody said you were," Ashley said soothingly.

"I tell you what, Jerrico. To resolve this issue, I will take you on the grounds and show you there isn't such a tree," Winniford offered.

Jerrico gazed over at her brother-in-law.

"I'm not insane, Winniford!" she yelled, clearly offended. "There is something utterly wrong with all of you people." She huffed, rising from the table and running out of the room with Ashley following closely on her heels.

Moving On

A week had gone by since the incident with the magical storm. Jerrico had refused to revisit the area where she saw the tree with its deformed branch. Correction, the tree which they all tried to drill into her head as imaginary. Jerrico knew what she saw, and it was as real as the eyes in her head. But through it all, she had to give Ashley his just due for helping her get back to normal. Ashley went out of his way to smooth things out with her. He wined and dined her, as he did when they were dating. He kept things as normal around the castle as possible. But with his family, he was certain another incident was just around the corner.

Months had gone by, and Jerrico was now living her dream. Her workload was hectic, but it was a welcome distraction. Sitting in the small office assigned to her at Taylor & Frost, she was enthralled in a major case her firm had been working on. Mr. Clydesdale was a prominent fixture in the community. He'd served on many boards and richly contributed to a host of charities. But sadly, his wife came up missing and he had been arrested in her disappearance. Everyone who knew the gentleman believed he was innocent, but Jerrico had found some disturbing discrepancies in their client's alibi. After much research, she decided to present Mr. Frost with her findings. Jerrico walked down the freshly waxed hall and knocked lightly on his door.

"Mr. Frost, do you have a moment?" she asked upon entering.

"Sure, Mrs. Covington," he said, looking up from his desk.

"I was going over the Clydesdale file and, strangely, some very important details are missing. I don't understand why this wasn't caught before," she said, opening the thick vanilla file she carried. The blood drained from Mr. Frost's face.

"Mrs. Covington, are you implying our client is not telling the truth? If so, do you have concrete evidence of such?"

Jerrico stood silently as she slowly nodded her head no. Seeing how upset he had gotten, she knew she had to proceed with caution. Jerrico nodded her head no.

"That's what I thought," Mr. Frost said, giving her a stoned look. "I'm busy here, so you can return to your office," he said, standing.

As Jerrico turned to leave the office, Mr. Frost said. "We defend our clients, Mrs. Covington, to the fullest, and I advise you to let go of whatever misgivings you may have.

"Yes, sir," she said, closing the file. She proceeded back to her office as Mr. Frost suggested, but letting it go just wasn't an option. Jerrico entered her office and took a seat behind her desk. File in hand, she flipped to the page containing the highlighted information that disturbed her. Something was wrong here, and she was going to find out exactly what it was.

Jerrico sat in front of the vanity table performing her nightly ritual of brushing her thick, shoulder-length black hair. Ashley hadn't joined her yet. *He's probably in the study with his family, laughing their asses off at my expense. The kinds of things that are happening to me don't happen to regular black folks,* she mused. *But then again, how many black folks lived in a colossal castle with a set of unnatural in-laws? And a peculiar husband?*

Jerrico pulled her hair into a bun and secured it with bobby pins. She didn't know why she'd even bothered. Ashley would just pull them out when he made passionate love to her. That part of their lives, which was as normal and as hot as the Sahara Desert, brought a smile to her lips.

Jerrico set the brush down on the vanity. Out of the corner of her eye, she noticed the drapes sway as if a light wind had just brushed by. She relaxed her shoulders and took in a deep breath. She wasn't going there again, so she ignored it. *The window probably is not shut all the way*, she rationalized. She continued her nightly ritual as she opened the shea butter night cream and dabbed it on her face. The drapes swayed again. This time, Jerrico paused. She slowly turned her head toward the window. The drapes moved again, lightly at first, and then they began to sway with more intensity. Suddenly, the drapes separated and a gust of wind blew into the room. Jerrico stood up from her seat, heart pounding as she walked timidly toward the window. She felt as if she was a leading actress in a horror movie, and we all knew how that ended most of the time: with the actress being torn to shreds by some maniac. The wind kept blowing as she approached the window. She willed herself to remain as calm as possible. *After all, this is a normal occurrence,* she thought. The window was ajar, the weather had changed, and maybe another storm was brewing. But normalcy had long fled Jerrico's world. Reaching the window, she found it completely shut and, just like before, the wind had ceased.

Jerrico sucked in a nervous breath and pulled back the drapes, placed her fingers on the bottom of the window sill, and opened it. She peered out into the night. She didn't observe anything out of the ordinary. The night was beautiful, as always, in Miami, except for the fact that all she saw was trees and the glow of the lights surrounding the castle. She had to admit she missed the glow of city lights and the bustling noise that came along with it. Since the castle was miles away from the city, the sound of crickets had met her instead. Jerrico shut the window, walked back over to the vanity, and sat down. She knew she wasn't mental. Weird things were really happening to her.

Jerrico peered around the master bedroom. She lifted her head up.

"I don't know who you are or what you are, but you need to leave me the hell alone!" she shouted to no one. Then the room went completely dark.

A pair of emerald green eyes dangled before with a glow. The eyes seem to hang in mid-air, like a puppet on a string floating, and it scared her to death. Jerrico screamed out in terror just as Ashley walked into the room. The room flooded with light, revealing Jerrico sitting with her hand cupped over her eyes. Ashley rushed over to her and kneeled down at her side.

"Honey, what's going on? Why did you scream?" he asked frantically.

Jerrico's hands fell away from her watery eyes. The room was fully lit. The wind was gone and so were the glowing eyes, right along with her sanity. Jerrico fell into her husband's open arms and bawled some more.

An Awakening Experience

Jerrico sat in bed with a cup of herbal tea in hand. Ashley sat beside her, concern etched in his face.

"Now, start from the beginning, honey, and take your time," he said, prompting her to go over the night's events.

Jerrico took another sip of tea and placed the cup back onto the silver tray.

"I was sitting at the vanity, Ashley, brushing my hair. I felt a light breeze blowing into the room. At first, I just ignored it. I wasn't about to overreact over some little wind, but then it started to pick up." Jerrico chimed. Closing her eyes for a split second, she continued, "I got up and made my way to the window as the wind continued to blow. But when I reached the window, I found it secured. And that's when the wind ceased. I opened the window, looked out, and found nothing usual, so I sat back down at the vanity. I yelled at whatever it was. That's when someone flicked off the light. Then, I saw a pair of green eyes dangling in front of me and I...screamed."

She fell back against the pillow, totally out of breath and weary from recounting the night's events..

"But honey, when I came into the room, the light was on and there wasn't an inkling of this green eye thing you referred to."

"Fine, Ashley. Your wife is crazy as hell. So put a straitjacket on me and have me taken away." She sobbed as she pushed the tray away from her.

Ashley removed the tray, placing it onto the nightstand. He sat on the bed and cradled his wife in his arms.

"Honey, you're by no means mad. But what I do believe is being in this huge castle is overwhelming to you. The little things that go bump into the night are common in this type of dwelling. And the illusion of wind is just the castle's way of settling."

"What about the light going out, Ashley? I assume that was an illusion as well?" Jerrico asked, pulling away from him.

Ashley let out a slow breath. He was trying to be as patient with his wife as he could.

"Jerrico, I've told you before. We all have experienced these kinds of things in some form or another. It happens, honey."

"So, you don't think I'm losing it?" Jerrico uttered.

Ashley rubbed the top of her hand and said reassuringly, "Honey, your mind is as sharp as a tack. I think it's your emotions that are on edge."

Jerrico agreed with her husband to a certain extent as she held onto him. Her mind was as sharp as a tack, and but she didn't believe for a minute what had happened to her had anything to do with the castle *settling*. Jerrico was determined to find out what was really going on in this castle as well at Taylor & Frost, and she had to do so before she really lost her mind.

Good Morning Love

Jerrico arose early the next morning, surprised that she had rested so well. *That herbal tea worked wonders*, she thought, swinging her legs off the bed. Jerrico peered around the room. She was alone. It wasn't an unusual thing to wake up in an empty room. Neither was it unusual to find Ashley in bed with a full set of PJs covering his body. Jerrico had seen her husband completed naked only a handful of times. Her husband had a hot body. Rarely seeing it naked would seem strange to anyone who heard about that, especially since they were still newlyweds. But again, this was Ashley's way.

Jerrico thought back to their wedding night. Ashley had stood naked before her in the semi-dark room. The half-moon cast a soft glow against his bronze skin. Her eyes traveled the length of his muscular body, bringing heat to her own. With one tantalizing kiss, their bodies joined as one. They made love until the sun rose. The next morning, she awoke to him fully dressed. Jerrico was snapped out of her trance by Ashley's presence. He appeared before her just as he had on their wedding day, fully dressed in a dark designer suit, looking as sexy as the day they had met.

"May I ask what that look on your face was all about?" he said, taking her into his arms.

Jerrico wrapped her arms around his neck and kissed him firmly on the lips.

"If I can get you out of this suit, I would love to show you," she answered seductively.

Just then, his cell went off in his suit pocket.

"Sorry honey, but I have to get this," Ashley said as he turned away.

Jerrico let out a disappointing sigh. Her fantasy had ended, so she decided to get dressed for work as well.

Jerrico's cell phone went off as she opened the glass door of Taylor & Frost. Juggling her leather briefcase, Chanel bag, and a cup of Starbucks coffee made it difficult to get to the ringing phone. Dana, the receptionist, saw her plight and ran over to help.

"I got this," she said, taking the coffee out of Jerrico's hand.

"Thanks," Jerrico said, fishing the cell out of the bag.

"Hello," she answered, a little winded.

Jerrico's face lit up like a lamp. "Oh, my goodness, Joyce, how are you?" she beamed as she retrieved her coffee from Dana and headed down to her office. Joyce was almost as close to her as her cousin, Vivian. They had met in the sixth grade and remained friends throughout the years.

Jerrico felt guilty for Joyce being left out of her wedding. It wasn't any doing on Joyce's part. The fact was, Jerrico had gotten married so quickly, she didn't have time to include her or any of her other friends in New York. She listened as her friend chatted. Once in her office, she relieved her hands of the items she carried and slumped into her office chair.

"Joyce, I miss you so much," she said, finally getting a word in.

Jerrico listened to the soft chuckle of her friend's voice. Staring at the calendar on her desk, Jerrico began to form an idea. It was two months before Christmas, and she would love to have her friend here with her to share the holiday.

"Joyce, may I ask you something?" she said. "How would you like to come to Miami for Christmas?"

"Are you serious?" Joyce responded.

"Yes, I most certainly am, and I'll pay for your trip. There's no need to worry about hotel reservations because you will be staying with me."

"You mean at the castle?" Joyce said, amused.

"Yes, at the castle. We have twenty-five rooms, Joyce. I'm sure I can hook you up, girl," said Jerrico, reverting to the street language they used when they hung out together.

"You're sure your hubby won't mind? I mean, you are still a newlywed, Jerrico," Joyce exclaimed.

Jerrico picked up the pen off her desk and twirled it between her fingers.

"Don't you worry about him, Joyce. He will be glad to have you. Anyway, I think I owe you this one. I feel so bad about you missing my wedding."

"Jerrico, don't you dare feel guilty about that. I understood completely. You found your prince and you hopped on it, girl. I would have done the exact same thing!" Joyce chuckled.

The truth was, Jerrico needed Joyce's visit. She needed someone familiar, someone she could confide in. Someone who could help her figure out these strange happenings. Of course, she had Vivian but lately, even she was acting somewhat bizarre.

"So, can I make the reservations?"

Jerrico held her breath as she awaited Joyce's response.

"Yes, you can, girl. I would be as nutty as peanut butter to pass on an opportunity such as this."

"Great! I will call you later and fill you in on the details."

"Okay, and sorry for calling you so early."

"I'm just glad you called, Joyce. I can't wait to see you."

"Same here, Jerrico," Joyce said excitedly.

The women talked a few more minutes, and then Jerrico ended the call as she heard a knock on her door. It was Connie Zimmerman, a paralegal from across the hall. She and Jerrico had hit it off on the very first day. Connie was a beautiful, middle-aged woman with hair as red as fire. She wore a truckload of makeup and reminded her of the country singer, Reba McEntire. Connie was down to earth and always to the point.

"Hey, kid. I need to talk to you," she said, stepping inside Jerrico's office and closing the door behind her.

"Okay, Connie, you have my undivided attention," Jerrico said, folding her hands beneath her chin.

Connie took the seat across from Jerrico. She crossed her legs, and the black linen skirt rose midway. Jerrico couldn't figure how she got away with it. Taylor & Frost had a dress code but, evidently, it didn't apply to Connie.

"I heard you've been kicking up some dust on the Clydesdale Case."

Jerrico braced herself for a long lecture.

Nodding her head, she said, "If you mean that I'm checking into some things, then I say you're right."

Connie unfolded her legs and leaned forward in her seat. She looked Jerrico directly in the eyes and said, "Kid, I know you're eager to prove yourself around here. I see that in you. You are a real go-getter and that's cool. But I'm telling you, as a co-worker and as a friend, leave the Clydesdale case alone. We've gathered all the necessary facts and will be going to trial soon."

Jerrico tilted her head and picked up the same pen she was playing with before.

"What's up with this case, Connie? It's like we're being blackmailed to keep quiet."

Connie looked away for just for a second. It was subtle, but Jerrico noticed.

Returning her gaze, Connie said. "Jerrico, you don't know who you are dealing with. Mr. Clydesdale is one of our elite clients. His reputation is golden, and we have to keep it that way."

"Regardless of the fact that he killed his wife?" Jerrico stated, placing the pen back down on the desk.

"Have you found evidence of that, Kid?"

As much as she liked Connie, the nickname of "Kid" had begun to get on her nerves.

"I believe he is guilty, Connie," Jerrico said, pushing back her seat.

"Kid, I hate to pop the air out of your balloon, but what you think doesn't really matter. He is innocent until proven otherwise, so you just need to keep your nose clean. These bigwigs around here don't mind getting rid of what they call pests. You don't want your career to end before it even gets started." The wheels were still turning in Jerrico's head. She wasn't going to back down and Connie knew it.

"Has a body been found?" Connie challenged.

Jerrico folded her arms against her chest and said defensively, "No, but that doesn't mean one is not out there."

Connie let out a sigh and got to her feet.

"Jerrico, clients here at Taylor & Frost are very different. They are not like clients you will work for now, or ever will again."

Letting her arms drop, Jerrico said, "Connie, I need you to clarify that statement."

"No Kid, that statement is clear enough. You're not working in a prosecutor's office. But I know you will soon figure it out. You are a smart one. Just take heed to my words and stay on your side of the fence," Connie said as she got up and walked out the door.

Order In The Court

A couple of days later, Jerrico had the pleasure of meeting the elite and distinguished Mr. George Clydesdale. His case was coming before the judge, and Mr. Frost had selected her instead of Connie as his paralegal for the appointed day. As they walked into the courtroom, Jerrico wasn't surprised to see that it was packed with spectators. This high-profile case had garnered national attention. Jerrico couldn't keep her eyes off the tall man dressed in a dark suit with salt and pepper hair curled upon his head and piercing emerald eyes that were set deep in his face. He stared at Jerrico intently.

Jerrico refused to let the similarities of his eyes to those of her new family distract her. Today was too important. The man's life was on the line, but his missing wife was just as much a concern to her. The woman had disappeared three days before Thanksgiving, when she went to the mall to shop for Christmas presents. The mall surveillance cameras had shown her exiting the mall around seven PM, shopping bags in tow. That's where the trail ended. Her car, a 2019 black

Infinity, was found in the parking lot of the mall, but Mrs. Clydesdale was nowhere to be found. After several weeks of investigation, the police finally arrested Mr. Clydesdale. He immediately made bail and proclaimed his innocence. Most of the community stood with him, with the exception of his wife's family, who thought he was as guilty as sin.

The Clydesdale's very own housekeeper of twenty years, Mrs. Ruiz, had said that she believed Mr. Clydesdale was guilty as well. According to what Jerrico read in the file, Mrs. Ruiz witnessed him standing over a large trunk in the basement of the home the very night she disappeared. Mrs. Ruiz had gone down into the basement to dig out the Christmas decorations Mrs. Clydesdale had wanted. When Mr. Clydesdale saw her, she said he panicked, ordering her in a loud voice to go back upstairs. She'd tried to explain the purpose of her coming into the basement, but he wasn't hearing it. Mrs. Ruiz said she noticed Mr. Clydesdale's odd behavior. In all of the twenty years she had known him, he'd never raised his voice to her, ever. But there he was, standing before her with a glisten of cold sweat beaming from his forehead. Yet, when the home was searched with a fine-tooth comb, nothing incriminating was found, and certainly not a large trunk. Soon after that, Mrs. Ruiz had disappeared. It was said that she had gone back to Mexico to be with her family, but when they notified the Mexican police department, it was verified that there was no Ruiz family living at the address given. Jerrico looked away from the paperwork in front of her and stared at the judge's head. There was a raven perched above her. The bird flapped its black wings and let out its familiar sound. Jerrico looked around frantically. It disturbed her that no one else seemed to notice the bird but her. Was she trapped, yet again, in her own psychosis? Jerrico blinked several times, taking in air to calm her nerves. It was evident now that she was seeing something no one else could see. The words *not guilty* rang out like a church bell, signaling noon. Mr. Clydesdale's supporters cheered with delight while Mrs. Clydesdale's family cried in disbelief. Jerrico looked at Mrs. Clydesdale's family and saw the pain etched in their faces. She turned her attention back to the judge and saw that the raven she had seen disappeared. She knew, without a shadow of doubt, that

a guilty man had just been set free and that she, herself, was
a target of evil

Sneaking Up On You

Jerrico placed her cell phone onto the nightstand. She'd made her friend's travel reservation. Joyce was scheduled to arrive one week before Christmas, and Jerrico could hardly wait. With a smile on her face, she turned around and peered into Ashley's emerald eyes. As usual, she didn't hear as he entered the room. *The man must have a secret float mechanism underneath his feet*, she mused.

"Ashley, why do you always sneak up on me like that?" she asked irritably.

Ignoring her question, he asked, "Who were you speaking to?"

Ashley's voice was even, yet cool. Jerrico took a lock of her thick hair and twirled it around her fingers. It was a habit she had when she was a little nervous. She knew from his expression he wasn't going to like her answer. The Covingtons didn't take kindly to what they called 'outsiders' unless they were cleared by the patriarch, Zackery.

"Um, I've made reservations for my friend, Joyce, to come out for a visit during Christmas. You know she missed our wedding and I wanted to make it up to her," she said gleefully.

Just as Jerrico predicted, Ashley didn't mirror her joy. "If you want to make it up to her, honey, why don't you just send her an expensive gift? You don't have to fly her here."

The glee left Jerrico's face, and annoyance had taken its place. With a roll of her head, she said, "Are you telling me you don't want my friend to visit me? Why do you and your family have a problem with visitors?"

"It's not a problem…it's just that my parents are very particular about who we have as guests," he said guardedly.

Jerrico's head continued to roll as she said, "Oh, so what you are saying is that Joyce may not make the cut?" Jerrico made air quotes with her fingers as she said the word *cut* and continued, "She's not swimming around in the circles your family is accustomed to. It makes me wonder, Ashley. How did I, a little known girl from New York, get in? Have they gone as far as having a background check done?" Jerrico raised her brows and waited for his reply.

Ashley let out a sigh. "If only you knew…" he mumbled under his breath.

"If only I knew what, Ashley?"

Ashley looked away from her and said softly, "If only you knew how ridiculous you are sounding."

"Well, help me sound sane, Ashley, because there doesn't seem to be anything that makes any kind of sense in this family at all," Jerrico fumed.

"There you go again, jumping to the wrong conclusions," Ashley huffed.

"I am taking that to mean I am always misconstruing things, yet again. Like all this creepy shit that's going on around here. Is this what you're referring to, Ashley?"

Ashley's emerald green eyes darkened. "I don't like it when you use profanity, Jerrico."

"And I don't like it when you and your family walk around here like freakin' ghosts either."

Ashley shook his head. "You have an overactive imagination," he said, walking away from her.

Jerrico pulled the lock of hair out of her face and placed it behind her ear.

"Well, tell me something, Ashley. Is it my imagination that I've only seen my husband fully naked two or three times since we've been married? Is it my imagination that you and my in-laws eat raw liver like it's freakin' ice cream? What is this thing you all have with blood? Is all that imaginary as well?" she said, folding her arms across her chest.

Ashley stopped in his tracks. He scratched his head, gave her a stern stare, and said, "I have traveled all over the world and, believe me, there are a lot of foods people eat that you are not accustomed to, but that doesn't make them weird. And as far as my body, would you prefer I frolic around naked twenty-four seven?" Ashley asked with a raise of his brow.

Jerrico nodded her head and unfolded her arms, saying, "Yes, that would be a natural experience, which is totally lacking around here."

Ashley blew out some air. "I am a very private man, Jerrico. I thought you understood that?"

"But I'm your wife, Ashley. Why should you hide your body from me, of all people? And it's not only your body I feel you are hiding. There are some things going on in this castle, and you damn well know it." Ashley winced at another word of profanity that came out of his wife's mouth.

"Stop it, Jerrico! We've been over this already and, frankly, I am tired of hearing it."

Ashley's voice had come out so forcefully, the veins in his neck bulged. Seeing him that angry sent a chill throughout her body. Jerrico peered into her husband's emerald eyes, eyes that drew her in like water in a desert, eyes that now were filled with agitation. Ashley sighed heavily. He walked over to her and cupped her face in his cool hands, hands that were never warm or cold. Jerrico's eyes glanced at the thumb of his left hand. She, of course, had long ago noticed the deformity of his finger. It was something she secretly struggled to get used to. After all, Ashley had said it was a birth defect. It wasn't long before she saw the same trait in his brother and their father. But now, with all she had experienced since being Ashley's wife and living in this castle, she knew it was something diabolical. But she never had the nerve to bring the subject up again. Not even now.

"Honey, I don't like it when we fight. If you want your friend to come for a visit, then so be it," he relented.

Ashley's voice had returned to the softness she had known. He kissed her gently on the lips and moved away from her. He floated toward the door. Jerrico watched his feet. She strained to hear one step, but there was none.

"I'll let the others know we have a guest coming for Christmas."

Opening the door, he looked back at her and smiled. This time, his smile did not reach his eyes. Jerrico was becoming very familiar with this look in the Covington household.

The Family Business

Winniford and Zackery were seated in the library, where the men of the family had gathered to unwind and to discuss business strategies and family interventions. Family Interventions were incidents that had occurred or had a possibility of occurring that should be dealt with right away. In fact, there was an important family matter on tonight's agenda. Ashley walked in and the men looked up.

"Hello, son," Zackery greeted taking a long drag of his Gurkha Black Dragon cigar.

Enjoying the finest cigar in the country was one of Zackery's nightly habits. It relaxed him better than a glass of wine. Winniford just nodded his head as his brother took a seat in the adjacent matching scarlet red wingback chair.

"I gather we are here to discuss the Clydesdale case," Ashley began.

"Before we get into that, I hear we have a visitor coming for Christmas," Zackery said, blowing out a ring of smoke.

The aroma of the cigar filled the room with its sweet scent. Ashley always hoped his father would one day quit his habit but, after hundreds of years of smoking cigars, he knew Zackery wasn't about to stop now. Anyway, why should he? Mortality wasn't feared in their whole generation. Ashley crossed his legs and retained his erect position. He needed to sound *in control*. After all, his father was like a God. He ruled the sun, the moon, and the stars. He also ruled mankind.

"Yes, my wife's friend, Joyce, is due to arrive one week before Christmas. I gather Mother informed you," Ashley said, staring directly at his father.

Zackery nodded and said, "Do you think she will be a problem, son?"

Ashley cleared his throat. "I don't foresee any problems. The women will spend their days at the spa, shopping and enjoying each other's company. They won't interfere. I assure you."

"I hope you're right, son. I shouldn't have to tell you what impact it would have if they stumbled upon one of our gatherings. You are well aware of the incident that took place with George's wife. We don't need a repeat," Zackery said sternly.

"Yes, Father, I'm very much aware," Ashley said curtly.

"Speaking of George's wife, this brings me to another concern, Ashley," Zackary said, leaning forward in his leather chair.

"Jerrico's involvement in the Clydesdale's case and, from what I hear, she is still searching for answers. The case is over now, and so should be her quest to find out anything more.

Ashley uncrossed his legs, leaned back in his seat, and cleared his throat. "Yes, I have already taken care of that," Ashley lied.

He hadn't traumatized her as his father had suggested to him earlier. In reality, this would have meant revealing himself to her in transition and scaring her into submission. Ashley refused to do it. There had to be another way.

"Father, I promise you I will keep everything under control. Winniford and I can handle this," Ashley said, peering over at his brother. "You needn't worry," he said, hoping to squash his father's concerns.

Winniford's brow lifted at the mention of his name. Ashley had always depended upon him to be his wingman.

When they were little boys, they played *Batman and Robin*, solving whatever mess they found themselves in. Decades later, the games were still going on. Just like with his wife, Jerrico's friend Joyce. Unbeknownst to their parents, there was a secret that only he, Winniford and Jerrico's cousin, Vivian, had shared. And it would be revealed in due time.

"I will keep a close eye on the women, Father," Winniford chimed in.

"I'm sure you will, Winniford," Zackery countered as he took another puff on his cigar.

His gaze went from one son to the other. His eyes settled upon Ashley's face.

"Your wife seems to have a special interest in finding that missing woman. If outsiders get wind of this, it can cause major complications for all of us."

Ashley had thought that part of the conversation was over. But evidently, his father had more to say.

"That cannot happen again. We came too close to a human war before," Zackery continued as he studied Ashley's face. He saw the struggle in his eyes. Zackery lowered his hand, placing the remainder of the cigar onto the glass, oval-shaped ashtray. Leaning forward in his seat, he said, "Look, I'm well aware of how much you love your wife, but it would have been much better for this family if you had married one of your own kind."

"But Father, you married Mother and she was an outsider," Winniford said in his brother's defense.

Zackery peered over at his younger son. His eyes darkened as he said, "But I *made* her one of us." His father's voice had changed. The words seem to growl from his lips.

"Yes, you did, Father," Ashley said quietly, "But I refuse to do that to my bride. It has to be *her* choice. I will not force it upon her."

"Well, be prepared to lose her, son. Independent women like Jerrico are not easily converted. They have no understanding of us in human form, and neither will they in transformation."

"Jerrico will understand me. Our love will survive," Ashley said, standing. "Is there anything else, Father?" It was clear to Zackery how upset Ashley had become. Zackery thought his son seemed to have lost a bit of his animalistic side.

Ashley's eyes met his father's stare with heat. As much as Ashley loved and respected his father, he loved his wife that much more. He wasn't going to let anyone harm not one hair of her body, not even his father.

Can't Let It Go

Jerrico poured over the Clydesdale file, although she had already been assigned to another case. Even though the charges against him had been dismissed, she just couldn't seem to let it go. There were too many unanswered questions. Yet, everything had been swept underneath the legal rug. Jerrico read through the paperwork once more. Mrs. Ruiz also reported that after the first incident with Mr. Clydesdale, she later heard several muffled voices coming from the family's basement. Although she was still frightened from the previous encounter with Mr. Clydesdale, she had gone down to the basement once more. However, to her surprise, when she reached the bottom of the stairs, there was only one person there and it was Mr. Clydesdale, himself. He was standing over the large, black trunk. Mrs. Ruiz stated she was confused. She was positive she had heard voices, but where had they gone? There was only one way out of the basement, and that was the stairs on which she stood. Mrs. Ruiz stated she was afraid. She did not confront Mr. Clydesdale; instead, she quietly made her way back up the basement stairs. Jerrico wondered how a trunk of that size could just up and disappear. She believed Mrs. Ruiz's statement of hearing voices. There were accomplices with Mr. Clydesdale on that night. One man alone couldn't have removed the trunk alone. And surely, someone in the area would have seen an elderly gentleman lugging a huge trunk around. On second thought, as affluent as Mr. Clydesdale was, he probably had the job done for him. Suddenly, a gentle breeze caressed the side of her right cheek. Jerrico flinched and looked up to find Connie standing before her with a lopsided smile on her face.

"What are you doing, Kid?"

Jerrico quickly shut the manila folder.

Returning Connie's smile, she said, "Um, nothing really, Connie. Just had something I needed to go over. But I'm done now. In fact, I think I'm going to go home a little early tonight," she said with a yawn. "I can use a long, hot bubble bath and a cup of Mrs. Lance's herbal tea right about now."

Mrs. Lance was one of the Covington's maids who had taken a liking to her. She was an older woman who reminded her of her own Nana Ruth. She was also the most normal acting maid, not like the others.

Jerrico picked up the manila folder and quickly placed it into her briefcase.

"Tell me something, Kid," Connie said, staring down at Jerrico's briefcase.

"What are you going to do with the Clydesdale file?"

Jerrico and Connie's eyes met and held. Jerrico lowered her eyes first. She had been caught like a deer in headlights. She let out a long sigh.

"I get what you told me, Connie, but I know Mr. Clydesdale is guilty as hell. He killed that woman, and he's getting away with it. I can feel it in my bones. It can't be over, Connie. Justice hasn't been served."

Connie held out her hand. With a serious look, she said, "It's all over, Jerrico. Give me the file and I'll forget what I just witnessed. If not, you leave me no choice but to go to Mr. Frost with this."

"Connie, please," Jerrico pleaded.

"Hand it over, Jerrico," Connie instructed with a stern look.

Jerrico let out another sigh as she opened the briefcase, retrieved the file, and placed it into Connie's hand.

"Now, you go on home, Kid, and enjoy that long bubble bath…and Mrs. Lance's herbal tea." Connie smiled as she headed out the door. The funny thing was, Jerrico saw Connie when she had left but didn't see her when she walked in.

Cut To the Chase

It was midnight. The moon glistened in the sky. The sound of the earth crunched beneath his furry feet with each ragged step he took. He wandered through the thick forest, like an animal searching for its prey, his senses heightened with the slightest movement. Ears erect, he scanned the area with his glassy eyes, focusing like a beam on the object of his desire. A silhouette of a woman appeared before him. be. He reached out to touch the figure, but she sprinted away like a frightened rabbit. Thus, the chase began. He, the fox, and she, the rabbit, sailing through the darkness of the forest, stumbling over damp roots and fallen leaves as they went. The chase finally ended as they reached the murky pond. The silvery full moon cast its glowing light upon them. Ashley shook the remnants of dirt out of his hair after his paws returned to their natural state.

Standing upright, he looked at the woman and asked, "Connie, what are you doing out here?" It's not your night to roam."

"I needed to talk to you, Ashley, and I think you know why." She growled as her eyes flickered in the darkness of the night.

"It's about my wife, isn't it?" Ashley asked quickly.

"Yes," she answered, landing her feet on the ground beneath them. She was now in human form. "She's been asking a lot of questions about the Clyesdale's case. I caught her this evening, sneaking the file into her briefcase. Of course, I confronted her and was able to get the file back. It's an understatement to say Mr. Frost is not happy about this at all. The outsiders cannot be brought into this, Ashley. It would be a catastrophe to our very existence."

"I know, Connie. My father has already made that perfectly clear."

"Well, I have a message for you from Mr. Frost. Silence your wife. If not, the Alphas will."

Then, with a blink of an eye, she was gone.

Looking For Answers

Jerrico parked her car in front of the two-story, Victorian style home. The home was located in a wealthy subdivision with tree lined streets and manicured lawns. Jerrico walked up to the front porch with its white columns that seemed to reach the sky. The red door loomed before her. Should she knock, disturbing the occupants with her suspicions? Maybe this was a bad idea after all. Hadn't she been warned to leave it alone? Jerrico turned on her heels to head back to her car when the red door opened.

"Excuse me, young lady. Can I help you?" a soft, but firm voice said.

Jerrico turned and looked into the eyes of Mrs. Clydesdale's mother. From the picture she'd seen in the file, Katie Clydesdale was the spitting image of her mother. Jerrico clutched her designer bag and walked back up the stairs.

"The old woman sized up Jerrico with one long sweep of her eyes. She pondered as to whether or not to let her in. What could she possibly want?

As if Jerrico had read her mind. she said, "My name is Jerrico Covington. I'm sorry to disturb you, Mrs. Wise, but I need to speak to you about your daughter's disappearance."

Mrs. Wise didn't respond, but Jerrico could tell by the look on her face that she'd piqued her interest. Mrs Wise held the door open and motioned for Jerrico to step inside. Mrs. Wise offered Jerrico a cup of tea, which she accepted. Soon, they were seated in the spacious living room decorated with antique furnishings. Jerrico noticed several pictures of family members, including Mrs. Wise's daughter, Katie, on the mantel of the fireplace.

"So, what is it you'd like to know?" Mrs. Wise asked, holding her teacup.

"Do you know, Mrs. Wise, if your daughter and her husband were having any marital problems before the disappearance?"

Mrs. Wise set her cup on the oval-shaped coffee table. She stared at her daughter's photo on the fireplace mantel for a moment, then returned her gaze to Jerrico.

"Didn't all of this come out in the trial, Mrs. Covington?"

Jerrico nodded and raised her brow. "Did it totally, Mrs. Wise? I feel there is a lot more to this story."

Mrs Wise hesitated for a moment. In a barely audible voice, she began, "My daughter loved George Clydesdale with all of her heart, but there was something unusual about that man. And to be straightforward, Mrs. Covington, it spilled out into his family as well."

Chill bumps began to form on Jerrico's arms and her chin quivered. She leaned forward and asked, "Could you please explain that farther, Mrs. Wise?"

Mrs. Wise looked up at her daughter's photo once more and then into Jerrico's anxious eyes. "My daughter told me she had been noticing odd things about her husband, from the very day they got married. But at first, she ignored it."

"Odd things. Could you be more specific?" Jerrico prodded.

Mrs. Wise retrieved her cup of tea, along with a silver spoon. She placed it in the cup and began to stir. The room was so quiet, it seemed as if the clinking of the spoon against the china spoke volumes as Jerrico awaited her reply.

"You know, you remind me so much of my daughter, Katie; so young and beautiful. Are you married, my dear?" Mrs Wise asked. Jerrico nodded her head and smiled. She did not want Mrs. Wise to lose focus, so she continued on.

"Go ahead. Mrs. Wise. What kind of things did your daughter notice?" Mrs. Wise exhaled. "Well, for starters, having the ability to appear out of thin air, and not being heard when he entered or left a room. And if I that wasn't strange enough my dear, having a fetish for raw meat." Jerrico's fingers tightened around the teacup she held as the old lady spoke. "Katie said sudden bursts of air would rise up out of nowhere at any given time. She also said she felt as if someone or something was watching her every move."

Mrs. Wise fell back against her chair and let out a tired sigh. She nearly spilled the tea, but her crooked fingers steadied the cup.

"George wanted her to think she was losing her mind, but I know what my Katie was going through was very real." Mrs. Wise perked up again as she held the cup of tea and took another sip. Leaning forward, she set the cup back on the table. "I confronted George a few days before Katie disappeared." She continued. "I told him I knew he was trying to drive my daughter mad."

Jerrico scooted to the edge of her seat. "What did he say, Mrs. Wise?"

"He told me to go home and leave what I thought I knew alone if I knew what was good for me. Shortly afterward, my Katie was gone." Tears welled up in Mrs. Wise's eyes.

Jerrico exhaled. Her instincts were right. Mr. Clydesdale had everything to do with his wife's disappearance, just as she had thought.

"I know my daughter is out there. I believe she is still alive, Mrs. Covington, and George knows where she is."

"You think he's hiding her?' Jerrico asked wide-eyed.

Mrs. Wise nodded her head and spoke in almost a whisper, "Dear, George and his whole family are very dangerous people. My daughter isn't the only one that has disappeared over the years, you know. There have been others, and they were all involved with the Clydesdales in some form or another. Truly, I don't believe you can even call them people. To me, they are really vicious animals."

"You're speaking hypothetically," Jerrico said.

"My dear, I am speaking literally."

Mrs. Wise's eyes stretched as wide as saucers as she continued, "The night before my daughter disappeared, she told me she had found something in that basement of hers."

Jerrico's interest grew even more as she hung onto Mrs. Wise's every word.

"Was it a trunk, Mrs. Wise?"

Mrs. Wise shook her head vigorously. "No, Mrs. Covington, it was a huge ice chest filled with hearts and livers…human ones. Can you imagine such an awful thing?"

The sterling silver-framed picture of Katie suddenly fell from the fireplace's mantel and tumbled to the floor with a thud. Both ladies nearly jumped out of their seat. Jerrico's started to shiver even more. It seemed as if the temperature in Mrs. Wise's home had plummeted to a frigid degree.

Someone or something is here, Jerrico thought, looking around nervously. Nevertheless, she wasn't about to stop now. She needed to find out more.

"M-Mrs. Wise," she stammered. "Are you absolutely sure about all this?"

Mrs. Wise got up slowly from her chair and shuffled over to the fireplace. She picked up the fallen photo of her daughter and placed it back to where it was.

"Tell me, Mrs. Covington, why on earth would I make up something so evil?"

Jerrico thought back to the case. According to the Clydesdale file, the house was searched from top to bottom. Surely, an ice chest filled with human organs would have been included in the report, but it wasn't.

"Mrs. Wise, why didn't you tell someone about this, especially the authorities?"

"I did, but no one would listen to me. They thought I was just a heartbroken mother grasping at straws, especially since George told them I must have gone a little senile because he and Katie never had an ice chest in the basement."

"Mrs. Wise, I must go now," Jerrico said, standing.

Mrs. Wise stuck her hands into the floral-printed housecoat she wore and gave Jerrico a thin smile.. "Have I been of any help to you, my dear?"

Jerrico nodded. "Mrs. Wise, you have been a tremendous help. I'll be in touch," Jerrico said as she walked toward the door.

"Mrs. Covington," Mrs. Wise said.

Jerrico stopped as her hand touched the doorknob.

"I believe my daughter is alive and George knows where she is. That, I am sure of. He loved her too much to physically harm her. He's holding her somewhere to keep her quiet. It's what I believe with all my heart."

Jerrico gave Mrs. Wise a smile of her own. "You'll hear from me real soon, Mrs. Wise, I promise."

Jerrico hurried down the steps. She walked over to her car and, to her surprise, she found a black raven sitting on top of its hood. It appeared to be the same one that was in the courtroom a few weeks ago. The raven squawked three times before spreading its wings and flying away. Although she was shaking like a leaf on a tree, she was more determined than ever to find out all she could about Mr. Clydesdale's wife and her disappearance. Jerrico was about to enter her personal journey of The Twilight Zone.

What Are We Going To Do?

Cecelia peered down at Jerrico's sleeping face. Her daughter-in-law was such a beautiful woman. She could see how her son fell for her at first sight. If only she could be submissive and resign herself to stay out of their affairs. But Jerrico was like a cat filled with curiosity, and there seemed to be no stopping her. You see, Cecelia knew all about Jerrico's little visit to Mrs. Wise's home. After all, it was she who watched her every move and took in every word that was said. Cecelia was the wind that knocked over Katie's picture, and the raven that Jerrico saw perched on the roof of her car. She squawked three times before leaving Jerrico in a daze. Cecelia watched the fall and rise of Jerrico's chest. She was sleeping peacefully, like a child. However, for her, it wasn't a natural sleep. Cecelia had placed a magical potion into her much loved herbal tea that Mrs. Lance had made especially for her. Ashley stood silently on the other side of the bed, next to his brother, Winniford. Zackery, their father, walked in and joined them. He stared at his sleeping daughter-in-law with glowing eyes. "What's going on?' he asked.

Cecelia spoke up, "Jerrico paid a visit to the home of Mrs. Wise today. She knows all about the ice chest."

"And it won't be long before she finds out about us," Zackery grunted. His eyes narrowed, but the glow still shone as he peered over at Ashley.

"We have to stop her, now, son," Cecelia said.

Ashley let out a sigh. "I understand, Mother, and I will. I just need for you and Father to let me handle this my way."

"And when will that be, son? Are we going to wait for her to go blabbing our secret to the world? Is that what you want? It will happen."

"She will not," Ashley scoffed at his father.

"How can you be so sureAshley? She's a very strong-minded woman. She's nothing like the others. You knew I had my doubts about her from the beginning," Cecelia smacked.

"Jerrico loves him, Mother. She would never do anything to harm him," Winniford defended his brother yet again.

"Yes, and I'm confident I can convince her, Mother. All I need is a little more time."

The shutters of the bedroom windows began to rattle. A whiff of air blew in. An owl was perched on the window sill. Winniford went over to the window, opened it, and the owl flew in.

"Mr. Frost, is that you?" Zackery asked as the owl transitioned. Bones started to form, and then natural flesh. Soon, it was the shape of a man.

"Yes, it is," Mr. Frost responded, looking around the room. "So, what has been decided about the fate of this young lady?"

"Absolutely nothing," Ashley said as he and Mr. Frost's eyes met and locked. So for now, Jerrico was safe. As safe as they would let her be.

Your True Colors

Christmas was only a couple of weeks away, but it was hard for Jerrico to get into the spirit of the holiday. Sure, there were decorations everywhere and Santas on nearly every street, chiming the bells of Christmas cheer, but the brutal cold and snow-filled streets of New York were absent from this season. In contrast, the weather was a balmy eighty degrees, and snow boots were replaced with flip flops and sandals. It was a culture shock, but Jerrico knew she would have to get used to it. She was a Miami girl now. In a matter of days, her friend, Joyce, would be here, and she could hardly wait to take her to all of her favorite spots.

Jerrico walked into the mall wearing a khaki Miu Miu designer short set with cork-colored sandals on her feet. She carried a beige Louis Vuitton bag. Sure, she was there to do a little shopping, but her ultimate goal was to retrace Katie's steps, visiting each store that had picked up the missing woman on camera. Jerrico didn't know what, if anything, she would find but she had to give it try. Mrs. Wise was counting on her.

Jerrico walked up to a saleswoman at the beauty counter in the Belk department store. She had blonde cropped hair with baby blue eyes and a nice, warm smile that turned cold when Jerrico pulled a photo of Katie from her bag, flashing it before her. Jerrico asked whether or not she'd seen this person.

"No, I haven't," she said, quickly shaking her head. In a cool tone, the sales woman asked, "Is there anything else I can help you with?"

Jerrico's breath caught in her throat when she noticed the woman's eyes. They were now emerald-green, and they were giving her an intense stare.

"No, there's nothing else," Jerrico said hoarsely, backing away from the counter. And if that wasn't weird enough, when she turned around, she peered into the face of her husband.

"Ashley, what are you doing here?" Ashley's gorgeous smile greeted her as he pecked her on the lips.

Ignoring her question, he said, "I thought I would come along and shop with you. After all, you always complain that I don't take time to, as you say, 'chill out and have fun.'" He chuckled. Stroking her cheek, he continued. "You're nearly accusing me of being a dud, so I'm here to prove you wrong."

"But how did you know I was here? We haven't spoken since you left early this morning," Jerrico said with a raised brow.

Ashley laughed. "Oh, I have my ways."

Jerrico stood with her mouth ajar. She had no idea how to respond.

"Well, are we shopping or what?" Ashley asked with a lopsided grin.

Jerrico smiled and nodded yes as they walked out of the store. With a quick look over his shoulder, Ashley and the sales woman's eyes met with an emerald glow.

After several hours of shopping and a ton of bags, the couple decided to drive down to Miami Lummus Park Beach, a popular beach for tourists and movie scenes. *Miami Vice* had been said to have shot there. The couple walked out to the sand for a while and proceeded on to finding a grassy area underneath a palm tree, shading them from the rays of the sun. Ashley had brought along a beach towel, which he spread on the ground. They sat down. Jerrico placed her head upon Ashley's shoulder. Love emanated from the couple as they held hands. Jerrico remembered how she fell in love so easily with this man. Ashley's eyes were memorizing. It seemed as if he could see to the depths of her very soul. No one had ever made her feel as he did. Safe, loved and fulfilled.

"Jerrico honey, I love you so much. I can never live without you," he mused. Jerrico scooted closer to him and removed her hand from him. She touched his chin with her finger.

"I love you just as much, Ashley, and I feel the same way." She smiled. She leaned in and the couple shared a passionate kiss.

As they pulled away from each other, Ashley said, "To be completely honest, Jerrico, I wanted this time to be alone with you. I know I haven't been available in the past few days. There were matters at hand I couldn't get away from."

"It's alright, Ashley. I completely understand."

Jerrico's eyes danced as she looked at her husband. Even though she was enjoying this romantic moment, secretly, she was happy that he had been spending a lot of time working on his projects. It gave her time to gather details about the Clydesdale case without arousing his suspicion.

Ashley also knew he had to address the real reason he brought her to the beach. He remembered his father's stern warning. He had to handle his wife. Ashley cleared his throat. "Your friend will be here soon, and I'm sure your itinerary with her will be full."

"Yes." Jerrico clapped lightly. "Joyce will be arriving at ten AM on Saturday morning."

Ashley looked away from her jovial stare. "You are well aware of the castle rules," he said guardedly. Jerrico stiffened, the smile she held slowly fading as Ashley leaned forward. "You practically have free reign of the castle, except the rooms marked with the number three. And remember, honey, no touching of the books in the library. In fact, I don't want you two in there at all," he said in a stern tone.

Jerrico frowned. Now, she felt as if he was talking to her as a child, giving out rules and regulations while her parents were away. Jerrico moved slightly away from him.

"Ashley, I can accept the rules about those rooms you've mentioned, but I don't understand why no one can touch the books, and now you're telling me to stay away. It's a library, for goodness sake. What are we going to do? Steal a boatload of books and burn them?' she said with a cynical laugh.

"Honey, I am serious. It's a rule that was made years ago, and you must adhere to it."

Jerrico gave him a mischievous look.

"For my curiosity, what would happen, say, if someone did pull out a book and open it? Would their fingers fall off, or maybe they would lose an eye?" Jerrico chuckled.

Ashley didn't take too kindly to her joke. His expression grew tense.

"Please take this seriously, Jerrico. Promise me you will not do anything to go against the rules." Ashley's tone matched his expression.

Jerrico folded her arms across her chest. "What is it with your family and all of these *rules*, Ashley? This seems so mysterious, if not downright wicked. Normal people do not act this way," she replied.

Ashley looked away for a second and then returned to meet her gaze. He remained quiet. Something was brewing within him as his wife spoke.

"I know there is something you all are hiding from me and, as your wife, I feel I have a right to know what it is, Ashley, and I mean now." Jerrico steamed.

Ashley looked away from her stare and peered out into the ocean. *Should I reveal the family secrets to her now?* He contemplated. He was afraid of losing her forever, but he had to do something.

"Honey, you are correct. My family is different. They have their own way of existing in this world, even though it may seem strange to some people. But we live and let live. It's nothing for you to worry about or try to figure out. Just be happy with me and we will have a perfect life."

Jerrico got to her feet. "I'm not buying that, Ashley. There is more to this story, and you damn well know it."

Ashley fell silent. His mother was right about Jerrico. She was strong-willed, and he had to be very fierce with her. He made a decision he knew his father would like.

"Alright, then," he said in a voice Jerrico had never heard before. His emerald-green eyes gave her an eerie stare. Jerrico's heart skipped a beat. As much as she wanted to know the truth, she now wondered if she was equipped to handle it. The sun was on its way down to give way to the moon, a full moon at that. Ashley knew he had only a few hours before show time. There was a ritual he was scheduled to attend, but right now he had his own ritual to perform.

"Honey, you were right all along. My family and I are different. I grant you that. We have customs the world would never understand. We love each other just as any other family, but we are very different." Ashley stared into Jerrico's eyes. "But there is a little secret that I must show you." The emerald–green eyes darkened.

Ashley's expression became solemn. Jerrico's eyes grew wide as her heart started to race like wild horses competing for the finish line. Ashley reached over and grabbed her by the shoulders. He began to change right in front of her. His human features faded, giving way to an animalistic persona. His breath took on a rancid smell as a deep growl ripped from his now odd-shaped mouth. A terrified scream escaped from Jerrico's throat as she struggled to get away from him. With her eyes closed, Jerrico started to kick and scream, but the beast in front of her would not let go.

Ashley opened his mouth, revealing ragged teeth. Just one bite and he would have her, but he just couldn't do it. He transitioned back to human form. "Jerrico honey, you're hurting yourself. Stop this right now!" Ashley ordered.

Jerrico's breath came out in spurts as she opened her eyes, looking wildly at him. It was her husband standing in front of her now, not the beast.

"What happened, honey? You acted as if I was a monster. Why did you react that way? I would die for you, my love. I would never hurt you intentionally."

Jerrico stepped away from him. She didn't know what had come over her. Had her husband just now turned into…a werewolf?

Ashley reached out to touch her, but she recoiled. Ashley raised his hands. "It's fine, honey," he said, dropping his arm by his side. He backed away and looked up at the darkening sky. "It's time for us to go."

Jerrico hesitated. She found herself, for the very first time, afraid of him.

"Ashley, something just happened. I saw you…you were a…"

"You've been on edge," Ashley interrupted. "I shouldn't have kept you out this long. But please listen to me," he said, peering into her eyes. "My family's life has nothing to do with ours. I love you and I will protect you always, but honey, there is one thing you need to do for me."

Jerrico held his gaze. "What?" she mumbled.

"You've got to stop looking for answers to things that don't concern you. If you can just do that, you will find living with my family so much easier."

Jerrico had heard that statement before. Just leave things alone. It was what everyone wanted. There was something the Covingtons and Clydesdales were hiding. It wasn't all just in her head. She was scared beyond belief, that was for sure.

"Ashley cut into her thoughts. "When your friend gets here on Saturday, I strongly advise you not to involve her in any suspicions that you may have. Remember, my family has a strong sense of privacy, and we intend on keeping it that way."

"Ashely, I need to know what's really going on and what just happened to me just now."

"There isn't anything else you need to know right now, Jerrico. Just remember what I've said."

Ashley headed to the car, and she followed slowly behind him. Jerrico now knew that Mrs. Wise's observations had been confirmed. These people weren't people at all, and it frightened her to her very soul.

Father was absolutely right. Jerrico will never be able to accept me as the man I am in human form and the animal I become in transition, Ashley thought as they headed back to the castle.

A Special Guest

Joyce took in the beauty of the majestic castle and its landscape. She felt as if she had entered a fairy tale as she walked up the steps leading into the castle. Mr. John was waiting at the door to retrieve her bags while she and Jerrico chatted along the way. Joyce took in the huge walls with old European décor.

"Jerrico, this castle is just like the ones I've seen in the movies," she said excitedly as the women followed Mr. John.

"Yes, it most certainly is," Jerrico commented.

"But I must also say this place is a little creepy," Joyce whispered as they walked down the long, dimly lit corridor. They soon stopped in front of the room she would occupy.

Mr. John opened the door, and Joyce's eyes took in the décor of the room. Royal blue and angel white colors welcomed her into the huge sunlit room. It was quite a contrast to what she had expected. Somehow, she thought the room would look more like a Princess room with pink décor bringing out a more feminine and romantic view. Mr. John placed the bags into the large walk-in closet.

With a stern stare, he asked Jerrico, "Will there be anything else, Madame?"

"I think we are fine, but thanks, Mr. John," Jerrico smiled. Mr. John did not.

"Dinner is promptly at six," he said as he turned and headed toward the door.

"I know, Mr. John. We won't be late," Jerrico said, giving him another small smile.

"Mmmmp, what's up with him?"

Jerrico waved her hand as she closed the room's door.

"Don't worry about Lurch. That's just his way."

Joyce began to chuckle. "You mean Lurch from *The Addam's Family*?"

Jerrico chuckled and nodded her head. Then she reached over and pulled Joyce onto the queen size canopy bed with its royal blue bedding.

"I want to hear all about your life back in New York," she said excitedly.

119

Joyce held up one finger. "You will, but first, I want to know all about this beautiful black princess who lives in a wonderful castle. My life in New York can't begin to compare to all of this," Joyce said as she waved her hands around. "You got to be walking on air, girlfriend."

"Funny you should say that," Jerrico said with a raised brow, "but I'm not the one doing the walking on air, that is."

Joyce frowned in confusion.

"Believe me. It's a long story." Jerrico smiled at her friend.

"Well, I'm in the market for long stories," Joyce said, getting off the bed and walking over to her black leather weekender bag.

She reached inside and pulled out her laptop. Joyce was a fiction writer and was always looking for a new topic to write about. Jerrico tilted her head and chuckled.

"Well, Joyce Middleton, I can give you a story that will make you a New York Times Bestseller."

Joyce returned to the bed, placed the laptop on it, and pushed the power button.

"Girlfriend, go ahead and make my day," she said with a wide smile.

Later that day, Ashley found the women lounging by the pool when he arrived home from the office. Joyce looked up and was jolted out of the relaxation mode she was in. The photos she'd seen of Ashley didn't do justice to the handsome frame coming toward them. *He really is a knight in shining armor*, she thought as she gazed into those emerald green eyes as he approached them.

"Who do we have here?" Ashley teased, revealing a charismatic smile.

Joyce was holding a tropical drink in hand, which she placed on the wicker table beside her. Ashley took in the red and white, two-piece bathing suit the almond-colored woman was wearing. She was very attractive with long auburn hair pulled back in a ponytail. Her oval-shaped brown eyes stared back at him. Ashley knew when his brother, Winniford, laid eyes on this bombshell, he would become putty in her hands.

"Ashley, cut it out. You know exactly who she is," Jerrico said with a playful swat, taking him out of his reverie.

"That's quite alright, Jerri. We haven't been formally introduced," Joyce said, smiling as she extended her hand. "I'm Joyce Middleton, your wife's best friend."

When their hands touched, Joyce couldn't help but notice how cool they were to the touch. *Does the man have a pulse?* Did the story Jerrico had relayed to her earlier hold some merit?

"It's nice to finally meet you," Ashley said, letting go of her hand. "Jerrico couldn't stop talking about you."

"I hope it was all good things," Joyce grinned.

"Of course, nothing else." Ashley smiled back.

He peered over at his wife, who looked good enough to eat. She was also wearing a hot, two-piece navy bikini, showing off her short but shapely legs.

"You're looking good enough to eat, honey," Ashley complimented.

In the back of her mind, Jerrico wondered if he meant that literally.

"Thank you, honey," she said, returning his smile.

"Well, I hope you will enjoy your stay, Joyce," Ashley said, giving her a Venus fly trap grin. He was certain that she would. After all, she had a free spirit about her. Something he wished his wife had.

"Well, I'm going to let you girls get back to what you were doing. I'm sure my wife has a full itinerary planned for you," Ashley said, peering back at Joyce. Suddenly, Joyce felt a cool breeze touch both of her arms, giving her goosebumps.

Joyce felt the coolness in Ashley's stare. It seemed to penetrate her body like an invisible beam. A cold chill settled over her. Ashley leaned over and gave Jerrico a kiss before walking away. As he did, the chill dissipated from Joyce's arms.

"Ashley," Jerrico called out, "Honey, after dinner, I'm taking Joyce on a tour of the castle. I think we will start with the library. After all, she is an author, you know."

Ashley's demeanor transformed from friendly to cool and perturbed as Jerrico flipped the designer shades onto her forehead.

He stopped his stride and responded. "I don't think that will be a good idea, honey. The library is being renovated."

Jerrico raised her brows and said, "I wasn't aware of any renovations."

"That's because you have plenty of other things to attend to, my princess," he said with a forced smile. Ashley turned and headed back in the direction of the castle, leaving Jerrico and Joyce with suspicious looks on their faces.

Treated Like A Queen

Joyce stepped out of the luxurious, modern bathroom after taking a shower and wrapped herself in a thick, white terrycloth robe, compliments of the castle staff. She had been treated like a queen ever since her arrival. The staff waited on her hand and foot, attending to her every need. Joyce walked over to the full-length mirror. She admired herself and thought about how nice it would be to live a lifestyle like this. *Jerrico really lucked out*, she mused. Joyce turned and walked over to the bed, where her outfit for tonight was waiting for her. Taking off the terrycloth robe, she slipped on a Victoria's Secret black bra with matching lace panties. Next, she stepped into the red designer dress with the plunging neckline she had purchased from Nordstrom when she and Jerrico went on their awesome shopping spree. Jerrico picked up the tab for everything she had picked out. *What a wonderful friend I have in Jerrico. No, that isn't correct*, Joyce thought. *Jerrico is more like a sister and I love her very much.*

Wanting to look as sexy as possible, Joyce carefully applied the makeup from her IPSY beauty box. If Ashley's younger brother was as hot as him, she needed to look her very best. Joyce smiled with a secret that was yet to be revealed. She slipped on the matching designer three-inch heels and trotted back to the mirror. Joyce decided to let her long auburn hair flow over her shoulders instead of placing it in a bun. She checked her curves in the mirror once more. Winniford had to be blind as a bat not to find her attractive tonight.

As Joyce stared at her reflection, she saw what seemed to be a shadow lurking in the corner of the room. She turned around quickly as her pulse started to race. She scanned the room slowly, finding nothing. Joyce ran her fingers through her hair and let out a deep breath. The conversation she had with Jerrico rolled around in her mind. Jerrico had told her that she saw things as well as heard them. But she never expected to see anything with her own eyes. Anyway, she didn't scare easily or, at least, that was what she was telling herself as she resumed her position in the mirror. Tonight was going to be a special one. She felt it in her bones.

Nothing was going to ruin it. Then she heard a soft knock on the door.

"Come in," Joyce said as she sprayed on a whiff of her designer perfume.

"Are you ready, Joyce?" Jerrico asked, stepping into the room.

"Wow, look at you!" Jerrico exclaimed as Joyce spun around.

"Do I look nice?" Joyce asked with a nervous smile.

"Girl, you look more than nice. You look like you're a model for Tyra Banks."

Joyce smiled broadly. "And, so do you," Joyce complimented as she gave her the once over.

Jerrico wore a black dinner dress with cutouts giving glimpses of her torso. She accented it with three-inch heels. Jerrico wore her hair up in a bun with diamond drop earrings.

"I'm hoping Winniford will be at dinner tonight," Joyce chimed as she grabbed Jerrico by the arm.

The ladies headed out the door as Jerrico said with a chuckle. "Nothing in this world will stop him. Trust me."

Dining In A Castle

As Jerrico had predicted, Winniford was seated at the family's dining table, along with the others. From the moment Winniford's eyes landed upon Joyce's face, he was smitten. The men stood up as the women took their seats. Joyce was seated right next to Winniford and he was elated. Cecelia, too, seemed memorized by Jerrico's guest as well. Jerrico noted how the family seemed to hang onto Joyce's every word as they all conversed during dinner. It was as if she had blended right into their perception of an ideal family member.

"Joyce, you are a lovely young lady and I am so happy Jerrico invited you here," Cecelia beamed. Cecelia wore a smile Jerrico had never seen on her face before. It was like a cat going after a caged bird.

"Thank you all for having me," Joyce said happily. "Never in my wildest dreams did I think I would be dining in a castle, of all places, with such wonderful and prominent people."

Even Zackery, who was known for his rigid persona, had a smidgen of a smile as he peered at Joyce. Jerrico observed as she took a sip from the glass of red wine she held. If only Joyce knew that her visit almost didn't happen because of this family, and now here they were, acting as if she was a blessing of some sort.

"Would you be interested in taking a stroll with me after dinner?" Winniford asked, turning toward Joyce. Everyone became quiet as they awaited Joyce's answer.

But for Jerrico, the invitation wasn't a surprise and, of course, her answer was yes, which seemed to please Cecelia and Zackery very much. Their son, Winniford, was very much in demand on the social circuit and, according to her husband's assessment of his brother, the reason he was still on the market was because the family had been very selective of his beau, which made Jerrico wonder where she registered on the scale with the Covingtons.

Joyce and Winniford held their own conversation separate from the rest of the family throughout dinner. It wasn't long before they excused themselves and headed out for their stroll. Jerrico didn't want to be hypocritical, but she hoped her friend would take things slow—although she, herself, attracted to her husband, fell in love and married him just weeks later. Maybe her real concern for Joyce was because she knew there was something to fear in the Covington household.

Winniford and Joyce strolled along hand in hand on the very path Jerrico had taken when she experienced the storm. And just like that night, the stars were twinkling with the sliver of the moon shining brightly upon them. The setting was perfect for a young couple to fall in love and Joyce found herself very enchanted, even though she couldn't help but notice how cool Winniford's hands were. *Just like his brother's*, she thought for a split second. Joyce was having too good of a time to worry about the temperature of his hands. Winniford had cast a spell upon her she couldn't resist…literally.

An Exciting Tour

The next day, the women toured the city of Miami, taking in the sights. Even though Christmas was days away, the weather never cooled. It was extremely hot. The women wore designer shorts, mid-drift tops, sandals, and straw hats adorned their heads. A couple of hours later, the friends ended their tour at the Cheesecake Factory, which was known for celebrity sightings.

"Jerri, last night was so unbelievable," Joyce chimed as she took a bite of the strawberry cheesecake she ordered. She had stuck religiously to her diet, but it was the holidays and she knew there would be foods she just couldn't resist.

"The Covingtons are very interesting people," Jerrico sputtered in between bites of the cheesecake she'd selected...chocolate. "But I'm telling you, there is a lot more to them than meets the eye," she continued.

Joyce tilted her head and studied her friend. "Yes, they are eccentric, but how can they not be? They are from a different world than we are, Jerri."

"You can say that again," Jerrico cosigned.

"I didn't mean no disrespect," Joyce said, leaning back in her seat.

"Well, they are not of this world, Joyce, and none taken. "Have you not noticed the coolness of their hands, Joyce? Not to mention, the fact that I've been married to my husband for almost several months now, and I hardly ever see the man completely naked," Jerrico said, slicing another piece of cake with her fork. "And then, there are those rooms at the castle with the number three on them." She leaned forward, narrowed her eyes as she looked at her friend. "No one is allowed in any of them. And that's not only the strange thing. The castle has a beautiful library with thousands of books. But not one book can be touched. Now, you tell me what kind of library in this world won't allow you to remove even one book from its shelf?"

Joyce nodded her head and replied, "Yes, I admit that is odd and I don't have an answer, Jerrico. But what I do know is that Winniford and I had a very good time last night." Joyce's eyes lit up. "He was a perfect gentleman, unlike some of the leeches I've dated back in New York. I found him very entertaining. In fact, he invited me for a night out on the town this evening."

Joyce smiled with a glow in her eyes. Jerrico knew Joyce was being pulled in just like she was. Jerrico contemplated telling Joyce about what she had learned from Mrs. Wise, but she didn't feel at liberty to reveal such information at the moment.

"Joyce, please promise me that you will be on your guard with Winniford. I just don't trust him at all."

"But you trusted your husband enough to marry him within weeks," Joyce said sharply.

Jerrico looked offended, so Joyce placed her fork on the dish and let out a whiff of air.

"You know I didn't mean to be nasty. It's just that he's nice, Jerri, and I like him."

Jerrico remained quiet.

"Okay," Joyce said, shaking her head. "You have to tell me more, Jerrico. What or who do you think these people are?"

Jerrico scanned the restaurant for anything out of the ordinary, but found nothing before she answered Joyce's question.

"Jerrico, why are you behaving this way?" Joyce asked.

Jerrico leaned toward her until their faces were so close that they could have kissed and said in a low voice, "I believe they are werewolves."

Joyce raised an eyebrow and said, "Werewolves? You lost me there, girl. Werewolves are not real, Jerrico." Joyce tittered.

Jerrico leaned back just a little, her voice still low as she explained the transformation she witnessed with her husband, Ashley.

"A man turning into a werewolf, Jerrico, is farfetched," Joyce said, shaking her head. "Jerrico, where are you getting this stuff from?"

"You don't believe me?"

"No, that's not what I am saying. It's just that, Jerrico, it's 2020. Do you really think there are werewolves running rampant in Miami? Not to mention, the concept of black werewolves. This sounds like a Sci-Fi flick, girl. Mmmm, maybe I should try my hand at writing a paranormal," Joyce mused.

Jerrico's expression was firm. "Joyce, please don't take this lightly. What I'm telling you is the truth. What I saw with my own eyes was real. It happened, and I'm getting closer to the truth of it all. I just have to investigate a little more.

Joyce finished her cheesecake in a matter of seconds.

"I think I'm ready to go now," Joyce said as she began to gather her bags. She stood up from the table.

Jerrico stood up as well. She took Joyce by the arm, her voice low. "You watch Winniford very closely. Check out the way he walks. Pay attention to how he enters and leaves a room. And Joyce, whatever you do, don't stare into those emerald green eyes of his too long."

Joyce reached over and patted Jerrico's hand. "I think you're under a lot of stress and you need to take it easy, girlfriend. And maybe lay off watching those thriller movies you love so much." Joyce chuckled.

"I'm not crazy, Joyce. What I'm telling you is very real."

Joyce gave her a nod. "Okay, if you say so. Now, let's get back to the castle," she said, removing Jerrico's hand from her arm. "I'd like to take a nap before my hot date with Winniford."

Jerrico knew, in that moment, Joyce was not taking her seriously at all. She feared for Joyce's life as well as her own.

A Visit To The Office

Jerrico was on holiday break from Taylor & Frost, but she had one deposition she wanted to review and she needed to go by her office to get it. Pulling into the parking lot, she turned off the car's engine. Scanning the parking lot, she noticed several luxury cars with custom license plates. Since it was the holidays, she expected only a skeleton crew of workers to be there.

Jerrico entered the building and trotted down the hall. Her heels usually clicked on the wax floor as she took a step, but today, she wore sneakers and dressed casually in a baby blue capri set. Her hair was pulled up in a ponytail with a white ribbon wrapped around it. The office was dimly lit by only the emergency lights. It was usual protocol for after hours. Jerrico entered her office, went over to the grey file cabinet, and pulled out the deposition. Opening the file, she walked over to her desk and dropped down into her office chair. It didn't take her very long to scan through the paperwork, make several changes, and sign off on the document. As she closed the file, her mind drifted to her cousin, Vivian. She hadn't spoken to her in a while, which was unusual for them. She tried calling her several times and left messages, but as of yet, she hadn't heard a peep from her. Jerrico reached over to the landline on her desk and dialed Vivian's number. To her surprise, she answered.

"Hello, cousin," she said with a smile.

"Hi Jerri, where are you?" Vivian asked with a cool tone.

Jerrico was taken aback at the iciness in her voice. "I'm at the office. Why? Is something wrong, Viv?"

Vivian's voice softened a tad. 'No, it's just that you should be at home, not at work, Jerri."

"I'm not going to be here long. I just stopped by to finish up this deposition. You know I don't like loose ends." Jerrico laughed. Vivian didn't.

"So, where have you been hiding yourself? We haven't spoken in days."

"Yes, I know. It's been kind of hectic," Vivian said vacantly.

Jerrico noticed the coolness had returned to her voice. She asked, "Viv, are you sure you're okay? You sound kind of strange."

"I'm fine, Jerrico, really. How's Joyce? I bet she's having the time of her life." Vivian chuckled, trying to lighten her tone.

"Yes, she is, and most of that is because of Winniford, not me. They have been inseparable."

"Well, that's great. Maybe Winniford has finally found his bride."

"No, that can't happen," Jerrico said a little too roughly.

"Jerri, do you have a problem with them dating?"

Jerrico fiddled with the phone's cord as she said, "Vivian, it's like I told you before. There's something completely wrong with the Covingtons, and now I believe I know exactly what it is."

Vivian took in a deep breath and let it out slowly. "I'm not certain you do, Jerrico. You are taking this thing too far, and you need to get it out of your mind. Why don't you concentrate on your husband and having those babies he wants so badly? Anything else should be out of that head of yours."

Vivian's voice had gone from merely cool to decidedly stern in a matter of seconds. Jerrico wondered why she chose to go there. Vivian knew her position on the baby subject.

"Viv, Ashley and I have settled this. And we are fine. What I don't understand is why you are getting so bent out of shape."

"Are you sure it's settled, Jerrico? Because I don't think it is," Vivian responded.

Now, Jerrico was perturbed. Vivian was sticking her nose in a little too far. She and Ashley were adults and very capable of making their own decision.

"That's enough, Vivian. Let's just drop this conversation right now before we say some things we both may regret." Jerrico exhaled, calming the anger that rose in her chest..

The last thing she wanted to do was ruin her Christmas spirit and, more importantly, the close relationship she and Vivian shared. Vivian's tone of voice grew dark. It was deep and demanding when she said, "Get out of that office now, Jerrico!"

"Vivian, why, what's going on?" Jerrico asked, confused.

"Now!" she repeated.

"Well, alright! I am leaving now. I'll phone you later."

The phone line went dead. Jerrico held the phone in a daze. Clearly, this wasn't her cousin's normal behavior.

The sound of dozens of bird wings flapping could be heard against her office door. This couldn't be happening to her again. Jerrico mused as she placed the phone back onto its cradle and walked cautiously to the door. Adrenaline pumped through her veins as she leaned against the door. Her breath coming in short spurts. Pure fear raced through her as the noise grew louder and louder. Jerrico debated on her fate. Should she stay inside or open the door and face her nemesis head on? She placed her hand on the doorknob and closed her eyes, a prayer formed on trembling lips. But then the commotion had stopped just as quickly as it started. Jerrico opened her eyes, twisted the knob, and quickly pulled it open. She stuck her head out. The hallway was empty. Looking down at her feet, a gust of wind began to circle around the bottom of her capris. It was the same wind she had felt when she stood in front of the window in her bedroom that night while brushing her hair. The same wind at the willow tree with its branch shaped liked the number three. But this time, to her surprise, she wasn't afraid of it anymore. It was as if a calmness came over her. The wind began to push her down the hallway, not forcefully, but more like a parent guiding a child through a crowded room. It was taking her some place, Jerrico observed.

The corridor bent to the left and then to the right, and the wind kept pushing until she was in front of the conference room where important meetings were held. And then, magically, the wind disappeared. Jerrico held her breath as she made her way to the walnut-stained door. It was ajar, so the voices were audible. Jerrico leaned against the wall and took a peek inside. Her heart nearly dropped down to the sneakers she wore. There stood her father-in-law, Zachery, in front of a crowded room. The entire law firm of Taylor & Frost was seated around the huge oblong table, along with the infamous Mr. Clydesdale.

What kind of meeting is this, and why wasn't I included? And, why did the wind bring me here to see it?

Star -Crossed Lovers

Later that evening, Jerrico and Ashley joined Joyce and
Winniford by the pool. Jerrico knew it was too late for Joyce.
She had fallen head over heels for Winniford, and there was
nothing she could do about it. She watched as the couple
gazed into each other's eyes like star-crossed lovers. Jerrico
had thought that Joyce coming to visit would give her
someone to confide in, someone that saw things as she did.
Now, all of that was out of the window. Jerrico believed,
without a doubt, the Covingtons were brainwashing her
friend. But what was their agenda?

"Honey, you've been pretty quiet tonight. Is everything
okay?" Ashley asked as he reached over and pulled a strand
of hair out of her face. They were seated on the edge of the
pool with their feet dangling in the water. It was a rare
occurrence for Ashley to expose so much of his muscular
body. And what a body it was. For the life of her, Jerrico just
didn't get it. She and Ashley had several discussions about
him keeping himself covered, and now here he was,
revealing it to a total stranger…her friend, Joyce. And to

think, he had the audacity to ask her to go for a swim. Was she supposed to pretend that he was now a normal man? Ashley's voice cut into her thoughts. "Where did you go today?" he asked lightly.

Jerrico knew her whereabouts would eventually be questioned. She didn't know why he wasted his breath to ask because she was certain he already knew the answer. She felt as if she was under a microscope, her every move monitored by the almighty Covingtons or something. Jerrico kicked at the water, making a small splash as she replied, "I went to my office. I had a depo to finish."

"Honey, it's three days before Christmas. That could have waited. Don't you think?"

Jerrico turned to face her husband. "I don't understand why you're making such a big deal about it. I was there for less than an hour," she said. Irritation laced in her voice. She decided not to fill him in another paranormal drama she experienced. Knowing her husband, he would have thought she was just having another one of her illusions anyway. Although this time, it was people in the flesh she had seen as well.

Ashley heard the anger rising in her voice. "I'm not making as you said 'a big deal' about it, Jerrico. I just want you to stop thinking about work and enjoy your friend's visit. How can you do that if you always have your mind on work?"

Jerrico looked across the pool and watched Winniford and Joyce. They were all smiles as they embraced each other.

"Seems to me my friend has her own distraction, don't you think?"

Ashley followed her gaze and chuckled. "I think the old boy might have found himself a wife."

"No, he has not. Joyce is not ready to be anyone's wife," Jerrico said forcefully. Ashley looked surprised at her outburst. She tried to lighten her tone as she continued, "I mean, Joyce has a man back in New York."

"Mmmp, well he must not be too important," Ashely said as they watched the couple share a romantic kiss.

Jerrico took her feet out of the water and stood up. She had seen enough of Joyce's frolicking with the enemy. "I think I'm going to turn in for the night," she said as she grabbed the towel she had brought with her to the pool.

"I'll join you a few," Ashley said, getting out as well. "I need to talk to Winniford about something. It won't take long. I promise."

Jerrico made her way back to the castle. Entering the foyer, she walked down the long corridor, passing two doors with the number three on them. The next door was the entrance to the grand library. Jerrico walked briskly by, but then she stopped. She had a sudden urge to go inside. With a turn of her damp feet, she walked back. She pushed open the heavy door and entered. As always, Jerrico was amazed at the sight of rows and rows of neatly lined books against the rich, brick walls. As her eyes traveled from one book to another, one of the books began to glow. Jerrico stared at it as if she was in a trance. The glow became brighter and brighter, beaming to her like a lighthouse shining out into the darkness.

Jerrico was drawn to the book like a magnet. She moved slowly across the room. The book was near the top shelf. The same one she wanted to read when Mr. John had stopped her weeks before. Being short in stature, Jerrico was unable to reach it on her own. Just like before, she found a step stool situated by the leather chair near the wall. She walked over and picked up the stool, carrying it to the designated place. Jerrico stood on top of it, reached up, and placed her hand on the glowing book. She tugged at the book to free it from its slot. At first, it wouldn't budge. She kept tugging until it started to move. Book in hand, Jerrico stepped down and opened it. She began to flip through its pages scanning its contents. And the book read...

Alphas and Betas coexist in the natural world. They appear as normal humans even though they have lived several lifetimes. They are known for venturing out at night, especially when the moon is full, searching for those they desire. The Covingtons are Alphas passed down from generation to generation. Betas are those that are bitten by the Alphas, which turns them into their kind, as in the case of Cecelia Covington. Alphas and Betas must continue to multiply for their legacy to remain strong. This is the generation of The Covingtons. Jerrico's eyes fell onto a family tree with photos of each Covington family member.

Her heart felt as if it would burst out of her chest when her eyes landed upon Zachery Covington's family.

A lump formed in her throat as she glided her finger over each one. Mr. George Clydesdale was Zackery's uncle. As she scanned farther down the page, she saw that Mr. Frost was Mr. Clydesdale's cousin, and so was Mr. Taylor. And her breath nearly stopped when she saw the photo of Dana, the receptionist. She was listed as Mr. Frost's niece. They all were related and, according to the dates, they were all decades and decades old. Jerrico's hands started to shake as she examined the pictures of Zackery and Cecelia's children, Ashley and Winniford Covington. Jerrico stared at the photo of her husband and her mouth went dry. Ashley was actually one 180 years old. Winniford was 176 years old. Zackery and Cecelia were more than 300 years old. Three blank spaces at the bottom of the page awaited photos. Under the spaces, it read *The Children of Ashley and Jerrico Covington*. Before Jerrico could turn to the next page, the book disintegrated right before her very eyes. Jerrico stifled the scream that threatened to release itself from her throat. She jumped off the stool and ran out of the library as quickly as her feet could carry her. She hoped no one found out that she had violated the castle's rules.

Jerrico ran down to the door of her bedroom and went inside. She headed straight for the shower. Discarding her clothing, she stepped inside and turned the water on full blast. She hoped to erase the images of what she had seen in the book. Ashley slid the shower door open and stepped inside.

Pulling her into his arms, he whispered, "I want to make love to you, my love, and tonight you will conceive." Ashley's emerald-green eyes glowed as he stared into hers. It was all too much. Jerrico went limp in his arms.

The Velvet Box

Jerrico awoke to a sun-drenched room. She stretched out her arms and let out a long yawn. She hadn't slept so well in weeks. Turning back the satin sheet, she swung her legs off the bed and stood up. A red velvet box sat upon the nightstand with a white card beside it. Jerrico picked up the envelope and pulled out the card. It read, *Jerrico, I know Christmas is only a couple of days away but I can't wait to give you this gift. It's just a token, honey, to show you how much I love being your husband, Ashley.*

Jerrico picked up the red box. She stared at it for a moment, letting her fingers enjoy the softness of the velvet. Jerrico walked back to the bed and sat down. She pulled the white satin ribbon away from the box and opened the lid. Her eyes glistened with tears as she lifted the sterling silver, heart-shaped locket from the box. She opened the locket. Her wedding picture stared back at her. The back of the locket was engraved with the words *We will always be together Now and forever.* Jerrico snapped the locket shut.

"Jerri, are you up?" Joyce said from the other side of the door.

Jerrico quickly wiped the tears from her eyes, hopped up, and placed the locket and its box into the nightstand drawer.

"Come on in," she said as she pushed the drawer shut.

"Jerrico, it's nearly twelve noon and you're not even dressed.

"Dressed for what?" she said, flustered.

"We're supposed to be shopping for our men today, so get a move on it," Joyce said, giggling like a school girl.

Jerrico gave her a blank stare.

"Jerrico, don't you remember?" she said, placing one hand upon her hip. "We said last night when we were at the pool that we were going to get them their presents today."

A line appeared between her brows. "Um, yes, of course," Jerrico mumbled. Her mind was in a fog. She struggled to put the pieces together. Then, she remembered the pool and Winniford and Joyce cuddling. "Joyce, are you falling in love with Winniford?"

Joyce's face lit up like the huge Christmas tree in the family room of the castle. "Make that fell, and you would be correct," Joyce said, grinning from ear to ear.

"But what about Jimmy?" she asked. "I know you and he have been off and on but I always thought you two would have ended up together."

Joyce took a seat on the chaise. "Girl, that's been over for a while now. I thought I told you that."

"Like I hadn't heard you say that dozens of times before," Jerrico said. Piece by piece, the memory of the previous night started to come back, giving her a strange feeling inside.

"Joyce, we are in danger."

Joyce rolled her eyes and said, "Jerrico, please don't start that again."

"I know you don't believe me, but last night after I left you two at the pool, I went into the library and I found this book and Joyce, you won't believe it," Jerrico said wide-eyed. She closed the space between them and looked directly into Joyce's eyes. " I saw pictures of the Covingtons, and they all are hundreds and hundreds of years old. That in itself is mind-boggling." Jerrico threw up her hands as what she'd said didn't seem to register on her friend's face. "Just wait. Let me show you," she said as she scrambled for her clothes.

Moments later, she was leading Joyce into the library. Joyce watched silently as Jerrico ran over to the book shelf. Looking up, Jerrico searched for the glowing crimson-colored book she read the night before.

"There it is!" Jerrico said, noticing that the book wasn't glowing as it had last night. "Joyce, everything we need to know about the Covingtons is in that book," she said, pointing. "I'll get it," Jerrico said, rushing over to grab the step stool.

Winniford entered the room. Neither woman saw him enter.

"What are you two doing in here? I presumed you girls were going into town."

Joyce turned toward his voice and trotted over to where he stood. She planted a kiss upon his lips.

"We are, but Jerrico wanted to show me this book," Joyce said impatiently as she folded her arms.

Just then, three Bombay black cats scuttered into the room, which surprised Jerrico. In all of her time at the castle, she had never seen those felines before.

"Mr. John must have left the back door to the kitchen open again," Winniford quipped.

The three of them watched as each cat jumped onto the brown leather sofa and began to purr.

"Oh yes, the book," Winniford said absently. "Jerrico, I don't quite understand. Why do you need to use the library's dictionary when you can Google any information you need in seconds on your laptop?"

He moved over to the step stool. Bending down, he rolled it in front of the shelf, stepped up on it, and reached for the book.

"Don't patronize me, Winniford. You know as well as I do that book is not a dictionary," Jerrico spat.

"Well, what do you think it is, Jerrico? A sinister book filled with directions on how to murder someone and get away with it?" Winniford guffawed.

Joyce joined in as well, which angered Jerrico even more. There wasn't anything she found funny about it at all.

154

Winniford pulled out the book and offered it to Jerrico. She walked over and took it out of his hand. Flipping through its pages, she found that it was as Winniford had said…an ordinary dictionary.

"This isn't it. I swear to you, Joyce," Jerrico exclaimed.

Joyce sighed. "Jerri, please, I thought you were done with these crazy theories of yours."

Jerrico looked back at Winniford, who had a smug look on his face. She walked over to him and shoved the book into his chest.

"I know what I saw, and I swear I'm not going to stop until I get to the bottom of it," she sneered.

Winniford watched the women as they left the room. So did Ashley, Zackery, and Cecelia, who were the trio of the black cats sitting on the couch

Transitioning back to human form, Zackery announced, "Jerrico will not be a willing participant. It's time, my son."

Cecelia agreed with a nod of her head, and so did Ashley.

A Christmas Festivity

The Covingtons threw a Christmas Eve Festivity the following night. Cecelia managed to turn the dark and gloomy castle into a Christmas Wonderland. Looking down at the crowd from the upstairs balcony, Jerrico thought half the city was mulling around in their designer finest. Everyone who had a title in front of their name, along with their wives and husbands– including Mr. Clydesdale and the staff of Taylor & Frost–was turning it up with the most expensive wines money could buy. Vivian walked over to Jerrico, holding a glass of Changyu. She looked stunning in the black and silver wide-legged pant suit she wore while Jerrico was adorned with a flattering, red flowing dress with a silver neckline.

"Hi, cousin," Vivian greeted with a welcoming smile.

Jerrico gave her a half-smile. She was still upset with Vivian over their conversation a couple of days earlier.

"I see your attitude has changed since the last time we spoke," Jerrico observed.

"Oh, about that," Vivian said, taking a quick look around. "I was having one hell of a bad day. I didn't mean to take it out on you."

"You took it out on me by shoving the baby thing down my throat, and practically ordering me out of my office. Viv, where do you get off?"

"Jerrico, I can't believe you are still upset. Look, I'm sorry, I was out of line. I apologized. Now, let's not rehash everything here." Vivian looked solemnly at Jerrico. "Jerri, it's Christmas…a time of celebration, so let's celebrate!"

"Don't Jerri me and if you want to know the truth, I long ago lost the spirit of Christmas, Viv. I know something is not right about all this, and you know it as well as I do. I feel the presence of evil all around me. These people are not who you think they are. In fact, I know that some of them are Alphas," Jerrico said loudly.

Vivian took a long sip of wine as she stared at her cousin. *The secret is out*, Vivian thought silently. "Jerrico, keep your voice down. You have no idea of what you're talking about," Vivian said through clenched teeth.

"I am so tired of everyone thinking I've gone mad. I know what I've been experiencing is absolutely real," Jerrico said, giving her a dismissive wave of her hand.

"You're talking out of your head, Jerrico."

"No, I'm not, Viv. These people are not human beings. Do you know what I saw at the office that day? It was my father-in-law and about fifty of those people you see downstairs, including Mr. Frost and Mr. Clydesdale. What is the connection, Viv?" Jerrico asked with wide eyes. "I think you know."

Vivian lowered her eyes. "Have you talked to your husband about this?"

"Ashley is one of them, so why would I talk to him?"

"I believe after tonight, you're going to feel a whole lot better about things," Vivian said, reaching over and giving her a small hug, which confused Jerrico.

Jerrico pulled away, eyed her suspiciously, and asked, "What's happening tonight?"

Joyce walked up to the two of them wearing a silver-colored evening dress with a grand smile on her lips. "There you two are. The festivities are about to begin and I'm so excited." She chimed."

"What festivities?" Jerrico inquired.

"The Meeting of The Hearts & Minds Festival," Vivian answered, giving Joyce a knowing look.

"Why do you two know about these so-called festivities and I don't?" Jerrico said, looking from one woman to the other.

"Jerri...I don't know," Joyce said with a shrug of her shoulders.

"Don't worry about it, Joyce," Vivian said quickly. "You go on. Jerri and I will be right behind you." Joyce walked away without saying another word.

"You see? This is exactly what I am talking about. I've had it with all of you. I am leaving this castle tonight and I'm going back to New York," Jerrico huffed as she turned on her heels and started down the hall. As she walked, her head started to spin and she felt queasy. Grabbing her stomach, she made it down to one of the guest bathrooms. She barely made it to the toilet before losing her cookies. After several hurls, Jerrico lifted her head from the toilet and attempted to stand.

"Honey, are you okay? Let me in!" Ashley shouted from the other side of the door.

She couldn't let him see her this way. With one look at her, he would know that she was pregnant and he would stop her from leaving.

"I'm fine, Ashley. I'll meet you downstairs."

"I'm not leaving until you open this door, Jerrico!" Ashley shouted once more.

Jerrico turned on the faucet, cupped a handful of water, and threw it on her face. She dried her face and hands and took a deep breath. Jerrico opened the door with a wide smile and said, "I'm ready for the festivities."

A Special Announcement

Couples young and old took the floor as the classical music played. Ashley held onto Jerrico as they swayed in step. Winniford and Joyce danced nearby. Vivian also danced near them with a tall, dark, and handsome man she had never seen before. The dance ended and Cecelia got everyone's attention.

"We have a special announcement tonight, everyone!" Cecelia said, taking center stage.

"Vivian and Max, come forward please."

The room exploded with the clapping of hands as the couple made their way to the makeshift stage.

"Winniford and Joyce, make your way forward as well," Cecelia continued.

More clapping ensued. The light in the room dimmed as the spotlight flooded the stage, shining on the happy couples with smiles on their faces. Cecelia held the mic with a grin of her own.

"I am proud to announce that these couples have decided to be joined in holy matrimony under the covering of Alpha-Beta Association."

The whole room erupted in applause once more. Jerrico couldn't believe what she was witnessing. *The holy matrimony under the covering of Alpha-Beta.* In that moment, Jerrico realized she was surrounded by what she had feared all along. They all were werewolves and somehow, they had gotten to her friend Joyce. She had to get out now. Jerrico stepped away from Ashley and ran as fast as she could. Pushing through the thick crowd, she managed to make it out to what she thought was the foyer of the castle. Somehow, the whole exterior had changed. The magnificent castle as she knew it had grown even darker than before. Looking around, she saw what she thought was a light coming from the end of the corridor. Maybe it was an exit door. She ran toward it, hoping it would lead her to the outside world. When she reached the end, she pulled on the handle of the door.

The door wouldn't budge, but Jerrico kept pulling with all her might. Finally, it gave way to what she thought would have been her freedom. Instead, it led to another corridor, one she had never seen before. Jerrico followed the curve of the corridor, which led to a tight passageway. A little farther down, a grey door loomed before her. Just like the last door, she struggled to get it open.

Tears began to fall down her cheeks as she cried out, "Somebody, please help me. Please help me!"

Suddenly, the door opened and she fell forward. Down and down, she went. Like a rag doll, she cascaded into the abyss. When she finally hit the bottom, everything went dark.

A Beautiful Meadow

Jerrico awoke feeling the softness of grass beneath her. She grimaced as she moved her now sore body. Luckily, nothing was broken except the heel of her designer shoe, which she removed. Barefoot, Jerrico got to her feet. Taking in the view, it appeared that she was in a beautiful meadow. Flowers of every shape, size and color could be seen for miles and miles. She took in a welcomed breath of fresh air. Jerrico wondered if she had died and gone to heaven. She saw a narrow path to her right. Not knowing what else to do, she started to walk down the pathway, slowly at first. Then, her pace grew to a trot. Yellow butterflies began to follow her like floating little soldiers as she proceeded down the path. Her legs grew weary after a while, but she had to keep going. Jerrico didn't understand what was happening to her or why. Her life with Ashley had started off so beautifully. Now, she was in the throes of complete terror.

As she trotted along, Jerrico reflected to the beginning of their relationship. Ashley had disappeared for a few days. He wouldn't tell her where he had gone or why. She should have known then he was hiding something. Still, she never would have imagined it would have been as sinister as this. Out of all the men in Miami, why did she have to fall in love with him?

But why not him, she mused. Ashley was as handsome and charming as they came. She never saw anything different about him except…his fingers, the coolness of his hand, and his ability to appear from out of nowhere. Most women would be looking for signs of infidelity while she had to search for signs of humanity. Jerrico stopped and leaned against a tree. Her breath became shallow as she slid down to the ground. Pulling her knees up to her chest, she began to sob. She was tired and filled with fear. Oh, how she wished she had taken her purse and cell phone. She needed to talk to her parents right now and her ex, Sergen. Vivian had told her she saw him with another woman, but did she really? Sergen vehemently denied it. Now, she knew she made a terrible mistake.

Vivian, the one person Jerrico trusted with her very life, seemed to have deceived her. And then there was Joyce. Even she had turned on her. There was no one she could trust. She was all alone, but she couldn't stop now. Wiping away her tears, she stood to her feet. She had to get away and free herself from this hellish nightmare. She continued down the pathway. Jerrico felt relieved when she saw what looked like a majestic house looming before her. *Finally, I can get some help*, she thought as her steps led her closer to the grand structure. Slowly, she began to recognize the home that stood before her. Horrified, she realized it was the same castle she had fought so hard to escape. The Covington castle cast a huge shadow upon her. It seemed to laugh at her plight. Jerrico began to sob uncontrollably. She made her way down the drawbridge and entered the gate; she saw several people standing in a straight line.

Their faces were slightly askew, but their emerald eyes shone brightly as they looked in her direction. Zachery, Cecelia, Winniford, Joyce, and Vivian stood like statues before her. The tall man who had been introduced as Vivian's fiancé was standing near the gate as well. Jerrico didn't see Ashley until he walked from behind the tall man. Jerrico waited for them to speak, but no one said a single word.

The wind began to swirl with a whistling sound. It turned and turned, becoming flesh as it did. Suddenly, the beautiful weather faded. The sun descended, giving way to dark clouds. Jerrico covered her eyes, hoping she was having a terrible dream and would awake from this horror at any moment. But she knew it wasn't a dream. It was a living nightmare instead. The wind slowed and Jerrico peeped through her fingers to see what was happening. She couldn't believe her eyes. She was staring into the face of Katie Clydesdale. She began to speak.

Katie said gently, "Jerrico, I tried to warn you so many times. You see, it was I who touched you at the tree that day. It was my eyes that dangled before you in your bedroom. And it was me at the office that day, leading you to the conference room."

"So, why didn't you reveal yourself to me?" Jerrico asked wildly.

Mr. Clydesdale seemed to appear out of nowhere. His emerald eyes shined like a beacon in the dusk. "She didn't reveal herself because she couldn't. She had to wait three hundred days before she would become a Beta. Yes, my wife was a human just like you, Jerrico. Now, she is one of us and you are going to be one of us as well. This is the day of your awakening!" he announced, raising his hands over his head. The others began to chant. Their voices grew louder and louder.

"No, I will never become one of you!" Jerrico yelled out in terror.

Vivian stepped out of the line. "Cousin, listen to me, you can do this. Just think, Jerrico. You will never have to worry about mortality. You will live on with us forever."

Jerrico shook her head vigorously. "No one lives forever, Viv," Jerrico said.

"But we do, my dear," Cecelia smiled, revealing those white veneers that now looked like sharp fangs.

"No, Vivian, this is not how it is supposed to be. I don't understand." Jerrico cried, moving closer to her. "How did you become involved with these people…these animals?"

Vivian looked over at Max and smiled lovingly. "Jerri, it happened right before I left New York. I'd met Max at a fashion show in Spain. We fell in love and he revealed to me what he truly was. Alpha Wolf. Jerrico, Max is Cecelia's nephew. And now I am a Beta. I've accepted it, Jerri, and I don't regret it for one moment. Neither will you. I will continue to watch over you, as I always have. Just trust me."

"No, this isn't right!" Jerrico said with terror-filled eyes. "We could leave, Vivian. We can go back to New York, back to our old lives," she pleaded.

"No, Jerri, we can't. This is my life now and soon, it will be yours, too."

Vivian reached out to touch Jerrico, but she quickly took a step back. "I can't believe you lured me out here, knowing that you were putting me into this nightmare. I would have never done that to you, Viv, never."

"Yes, Jerri, I admit it. I did get you here for my own selfish reasons. But as I told you before, I wanted what was best for you."

"And who gives you the right to say that this is best for me?" Jerrico bellowed as she looked around like a caged animal.

"It is, Jerri," Vivian responded.

Jerrico began to pace with arms flaring and tears running down her cheeks.

"I can't believe you think becoming a Beta is what's best for me. I don't want this, Viv. I want to be who I am, and that is human!" She cried.

"Jerri, open your mind and you will see that this is so much better than living the life of the humanoids. You will never have to worry about anything ever again. Your life will be magical. Please trust me, Jerri."

Jerrico watched in awe as the people standing before her transformed one by one. Their faces, hands, and feet began to grow hair. Soon, their bodies were fully covered with it. Jerrico was looking into the faces of werewolves. She let out a gut-wrenching scream. Their animalistic eyes stared at her, and growling sounds came from their lips. Their growls grew louder and louder, so much so she cupped her hands over her ears. Moments later, they transitioned back to human form.

Jerrico removed her hands from her ears and took off in the direction from which she came, but it was too late. Ashley caught up with her and scooped her up into his now human arms.

"Let go of me, Ashley!" she pleaded as she struggled to get away from him. Jerrico thought about the night on the beach, when she was in the same predicament. Was it Deja vu? No, this was reality and this had become her fate.

"Jerrico, listen to me," he said as he held her in a tight grip. "I wanted to tell you all of this long ago, but deep down inside, I knew you would have never willingly agreed to become one of us. You were too headstrong and I couldn't take the chance of losing you, Jerrico. You are everything to me, and I want you in my world forever."

Jerrico stopped struggling and Ashley lowered his arms, letting her bare feet touch the soft ground. Jerrico stood before him with a twisted look on her face.

"So, you took it upon yourself to deceive me, your own wife. Yet, you continue to profess your love for me. I should have left you at the very first sign of this nightmare."

"You couldn't if you wanted to," Ashley said in a voice barely audible.

"What did you say, Ashley?" Jerrico asked.

"Jerrico, you were chosen for me. From the very first day you arrived in Miami, I was here waiting for you. Waiting to bring you into our pack."

"He's telling the truth, Jerri," Vivian said as she walked over to the couple.

"I chose you for him a long time ago. I'm the one who is responsible for the break-up between you and Sergen. He never cheated on you, Jerri."

Jerrico gasped in disbelief. She was right about her.

Vivian continued, " I tried to convince Sergen to convert and become one of us but, like you, he refused. He threatened to tell the outsiders all about us, but instead of killing him and taking his heart and liver, I chose another way. I didn't harm him. I set him up just so you could let him go, Jerri. I knew how much you cared about him, that's why he is now in a delusional state in the mental ward."

"Oh my God, Vivian. You are pure evil!!" Jerrico cried out. Her knees felt as if they would buckle from the weight of these revelations.

"No Jerrico, I am immortal. So, you see, Jerri. It was all planned."

"Yes, Jerrico, it was," Joyce said, stepping forward.

"You knew all about this as well, Joyce?" Jerrico whimpered.

"Yes, I have been dating Winniford for months but I couldn't tell you."

But...you were my best friend. I...invited you here."

"No, I was coming anyway, Jerrico, for the festivities, remember? I have become a Beta, thanks to Winniford and Vivian. Your cousin was the one who introduced me to him, just like she had done for you with Ashley. Only I accepted this fate...it's not a bad thing, Jerri. It's just like Ashley told me it would be," Joyce said as Winniford came and stood by her side.

"Yes, Ashley knew all about me and Winniford," Joyce said as her eyes turned emerald-green.

The wind started to blow again and a howling sound filled the air.

"As you can see, Jerrico, we were all waiting for you to complete our family's pack," Ashley grunted as he went into transformation once again. And so did the others.

"Ashley, please don't do this. Let me go!" Jerrico pleaded with her arms raised above her head.

"Welcome home, my love," he growled as he bit into her smooth flesh. His blood and hers intertwined as he took out her heart and liver.

EPILOGUE

A handsome couple strolled through Lummus Park. It was a beautiful Saturday morning boasting of blue skies filled with puffy clouds and warm breezes coming from the ocean side. There were families scattered about enjoying themselves in the fine weather as they frolicked upon the sand. Ashley and Jerrico Covington were happy with their new life. Everything had fallen perfectly into place. The couple kept walking until they found the same palm tree they had visited one year ago. They stopped their stroll. Ashley guided the carriage he pushed underneath the tree. Jerrico bent down and lifted up the top of the carriage. She smiled with delight as six sets of emerald green eyes stared up at her. They were her and Ashley's children. Ashley Zackery, Winston Alfred, and Jacqueline Lynn, The Triplets

THE END

Rehoboam answered, come to me in three days, so the
people went away.
  2 Chronicles 10:5

To submit a manuscript to be considered,

email us at

submissions@majorkeypublishing.com

Be sure to <u>LIKE</u> our Major Key Publishing
page on Facebook!

CPSIA information can be obtained
at www.ICGtesting.com
Printed in the USA
LVHW092036061120
670968LV00007B/1060